The Alpha's Mate Who Cried Wolf

Book One of The Alpha Series

Jazz Ford

Jazz Ford

Jazz Ford

Copyright © 2021 Jazz Ford

All rights reserved.

ISBN: 978-0-6452231-0-1

Jazz Ford

DEDICATION
....
I dedicate this book to my beloved husband, Steve Ford
'Omnia Vincit Amor'

Jazz Ford

CHAPTER 1

I push myself up from the floor and wipe the blood from my split lip in pain—my bruised eye swelling.

'Please, no more, Dad. Mum wouldn't want this. She wouldn't want you hurting me like this,' I plead.

'You should have thought about that before you killed your mother!' He shouts.

'Please, Dad! You know it was an accident. I didn't mean for her to die!' I plead. We stare at each other with cold consternation. 'Please, Dad! Please forgive me,' I beg.

He looks at me with hatred in his eyes before his expression changes. He smirks.

'Oh, Astrid, you're no daughter of mine! You never were: your mother told me your birth father died when she was pregnant with you. However, I loved your mother so much I was willing to pretend to be your father!'

'No! That's not true! Mum would never keep something like that from me!' I yell.

'Your mother didn't want you to find out the truth until you were eighteen. She wanted you to live a normal life. She said you would find your true identity once you were eighteen. I didn't know what she meant. I guess she was planning to tell you about your biological father then. You'll never find out who he is now!' He chuckles before kicking me in the ribs. I yell out in pain and hold my side. Locking my bedroom door behind him, he leaves me in my bedroom alone.

Dragging myself across the cold, hard floor, I carefully lift myself onto my quilted bed and lie on my side. I feel my broken rib under my clothing and burst into tears, not understanding how the man that once loved me and helped raise me could do this to me. I remember sitting on his lap in front of the fire when I was a small child. My mother would lean in the doorway and smile. She was so beautiful, and I loved I had the same green eyes as her.

I don't know how long I lie there this way before I fall asleep. The following day, I awkwardly pull my work uniform on and quietly creep down the stairs. Dad is asleep, most likely passed out in a drunken stupor. I pull my hoodie over my head, walk out the front door, and walk to work.

I used to go to school until my teachers saw the bruises on my arms and called Dad into the principal's office to question him. I begged my teachers not to contact him. They didn't believe me when I told them I was just clumsy and fell down the stairs. I haven't been allowed to return to school since I had to find a job as a kitchen hand and a server at a diner about a thirty-minute walk from home.

On my way to work, a black Mercedes moves conspicuously behind me. I have noticed this same car following me for a few months now. The driver is always watching me. I usually veer off the road when it approaches, choosing the longer route to work through the woods. I enjoy my job and my colleagues. My boss Jim is charming. He always knows something isn't right but never makes me talk about it. His offer to help is always there, unspoken, supportive and noted.

I walk into the kitchen and wash my hands to prep the salads and other food. Then, feeling too flustered, I walk over to where I left my bag on a stool, discarding my hoodie onto it and unzipping my jumper to cool down. Twenty minutes pass when Jim comes in to cook the first food orders for the day. A growl erupts. He sounds strangely like a wild animal. I look up at Jim, who isn't thrilled.

'Astrid, you know you can come to me for help, don't you? You don't have to go back home if you're not safe. I have friends in a nearby town who could look after you?' he offers.

'Thank you, but I'm fine. I just fell down the stairs. Jim gets a small smile from me.

'You said the same thing last time, Astrid...' he says.

'What can I say? My house is old. The stairs are rotting,' I say, bursting into tears and slamming my hands onto the prep table. Jim comes over to me, pulls me into his chest, and wraps his arms around me while I cry.

'Let me help you, Astrid.' he says. I stand back and shake my head.

'You don't understand. I can't accept your help.'

'Why not?' he asks.

'Dad won't let me go easy. He would rather have me dead and kill anyone who tries to help me. He hurts me because I am responsible for my mother's death,' I explain, wiping my tears from my face.

'Regardless of whether you are the reason for your mother's death. You don't deserve this. There has to be something I can do to help you, Astrid?'

'I know I don't deserve this, but I don't know what else to do. If you can't handle seeing a couple of bruises, I could always find a job elsewhere?' I offer and walk back to the prep table. I pick up the knife and start slicing the lettuce.

'I want you to stay, Astrid. I don't like seeing humans treating our kind like this, even if you are a rogue.' he frowns.

Pausing, with a confused expression, I stare at him.

'Humans? A rogue? I don't know what planet you're from or what kind of human you think I am, but we're all just humans,' I say and continue to chop some carrots on a blue chopping board.

Jim stands there in silence. I look at him and ask what his problem is now. He stands there looking very pale with his mouth open, completely frozen.

'Jim? Are you ok? What's wrong? Is it a heart attack?' I ask, walking over to him, concerned.

He blinks and goes to put his hand on my shoulder before I flinch and take a step back. I know Jim would never hurt me. I'm just not comfortable being touched. He frowns.

'I'm sorry. I didn't mean to frighten you,' Jim says.

'I know you wouldn't hurt me. I'm just not used to the gentleness,' I confess. Jim gives me a sad smile.

'Do you not know what you are?' He asks, on the verge of telling me something I sense I should already know.

'What I am? I don't understand the question. I am what

we all are. Human,' I say, giving him a weird look.

'Can't you even smell the difference?' He asks me. I laugh.

'The only thing I smell around here is the food burning in the frying pan,' I chuckle.

'Shit!' He runs to the stove to turn it off and removes the smoking frying pan.

We remain silent in the kitchen and focus on prepping and cooking orders.

'For what it's worth, Astrid, whatever happened to your mother, I'm sure she wouldn't want you blaming yourself for her death. I'm sure she would not want your father hurting you all these years because of it.

'Stepfather,' I correct him.

'Your stepfather? I thought--' he says before I cut him off.

'Yes, I only found out myself last night.' I explain that my birth father died when my mother was pregnant with me.

'I'm so sorry.' He looks downcast.

'I was sorry at first, too, but I don't know now. Maybe it might be a good thing he isn't my real father,' I say. Jim nods and smiles.

'Do you think you could work late tonight? I have important people coming from the next town for an important meeting. It would be great if I could join the meeting for a change, instead of serving the food and drinks,' he explains.

'I'll have to ring Dad and ask, but I'm sure he will agree if it means more booze money for him.'

My Dad says I can work the extra few hours. All my money from work always goes into his account, anyway. Of course, I don't get to see any of it, but I'd still rather be at work if it means not being near him.

'It's fine. Dad says I can work the few extra hours,' I say. He gives me a wink and a smile.

'Good,' he exhales with relief.

A few hours later, I have prepped food for the customers coming to the diner for their meeting.

'Is there anything I need to know about this meeting?' I ask Jim.

'We're just having some problems in Shadow Crest,' he

says.

'Oh, in Shadow Crest? I've never been there before. I've heard it's full of aggressive people who act like wild animals. Jim lets out a laugh.

'It's not that bad, and I live there. Am I aggressive? Do I run around like a wild animal?' He asks.

'Good point. No, you aren't aggressive. And, no, you don't run around like a wild animal. Not that I know of anyway,' I giggle. Jim laughs.

'If only you knew, Astrid.' he says, laughing.

'They will be here any minute. Just take everyone's drink order, serve my friends and bring out the food platter when you're ready.'

'Sure thing, boss,' I reply with a smile. 'Oh, and Jim, I hope you don't mind if I wear my hood up? I don't want to be stared at or questioned about the umm, split lip, and bruise...' Jim gives me a nod.

'Of course, that's fine.'

A short while later, I hear the engines of several cars approach and then park in unison, and several car doors slam. The doorbell on the diner door clangs loudly every time someone comes in. I stand on my tippy toes to see over the kitchen ledge into the dining room. There must be about eighteen men littered about the place. Not ordinary-looking men either. These men are big, bulky, extremely masculine, and ripped. They're all wearing suits and are extremely handsome.

When a very handsome guy walks in, everyone else moves out of his way as though he is someone significant. He has dark hair and gorgeous blue eyes. He is masculine, and his lips when he smiles - don't get me started on his full lips - all I want to know is what they would feel like against mine.

The handsome man sniffs a waft of something in the air and raises an eyebrow with interest.

'Jim, what is that smell?' He asks, looking in my direction. 'It smells like vanilla and cookies,' he says, still looking in my direction. I reflexively duck down and go back to finishing the platter for these handsome creatures.

'If you men want to make your way to the kitchen

counter, Astrid will take your order. But, please, no one freak out - especially you, Alpha Ryker, when I tell you, Astrid is a rogue, that's what the strange smell is,' Jim explains.

'WHAT?' Alpha Ryker shouts, slamming his fist on the table.

'Alpha Ryker. Settle down! She is just a young girl who needs a job. She has been under my employment for almost a year now and is one of my best workers. We're also not in your territory, so she isn't trespassing. She has done nothing wrong. So, I suggest you sit down and behave!' Jim warns.

'Are you threatening me, Jim?' Alpha Ryker asks.

'Of course not, Alpha. I'm just reminding you. As much as you and everyone here hates rogues, she has done nothing wrong and will remain out of all this. Alpha Ryker growls.

Jazz Ford

CHAPTER 2

Quietly preparing the platter, I hear a loud thump. Someone is angry. I'm just glad I'm in here and not out there with all that commotion. I pull my hood up to hide my bruised eye. Unfortunately, I can't cover my split lip, so I figure I'll bite over my lip to hide it when needed.

After approaching the counter, I ask the first man for his order. I avoid eye contact and keep my head down as I write them down. All these guys sound very grumpy and annoyed. Then, finally, Jim comes over to me.

'Alpha, I mean Ryker, would like a vanilla milkshake with some cookies.' I nod and write the order. I have served everyone except for Ryker.

Lifting an enormous platter of biscuits and dips, I wince with the weight in one hand. My broken rib is under strain. Ryker stares at me.

Pausing for a moment, I inhale a deep breath, hold it, brace myself for the pain, lift the platter again, and put it on the table where most men sit. In the kitchen, I exhale while keeping my hand pressed against my ribs. *Darn! Ryker's order.* Quickly walking to him to serve his order, he stares directly at me and squints, wondering what or who is under my hood.

All the other men are shouting over each other about some guy named Zenith, a town called Shady Crest, and something about rogues, which is strange because Jim referred to me as a rogue earlier. A map sprawls across the table in front of Ryker. The men are drawing circles and squiggly lines on various parts of it and talking about setting up posts here and there.

As the diner becomes quiet and all eyes are on me, I suddenly feel nervous. I can sense them on me. I nervously place Ryker's order on the table next to the map.

'Your order, sir,' I whisper.

'Wait,' Ryker says before I can leave his table. 'What is wrong with your ribs?' Ryker asks.

'Nothing, sir,' I reply, wondering how he knew I was in pain.

'You struggled to hold the platter. It's causing you pain,' he observes.

'I want you to remove your hood, rogue!' He demands. I freeze and look at Jim for help.

'Astrid, have your break, love. Ryker, I told you to leave her out of all this.' I run to the kitchen and out the back door.

'She should smell like a rogue if she is a rogue. But she smells sweet and sugary,' Alpha Ryker declares.

'You need to leave her alone,' Jim says. Alpha Ryker lets out a growl and glares at Jim.

'I could smell her before she served me. My wolf is extremely restless right now. I'm struggling to keep him back,' Ryker explains, holding his chest.

Everyone in the diner freezes and looks at each other, then at Alpha Ryker.

'What?' Alpha Ryker asks. His Beta, Seth, stands up.

'Alpha, you don't seriously think *she* could be your mate?' Seth asks. Alpha Ryker laughs.

'The Moon Goddess matching an Alpha and a rogue? Don't be ridiculous,' Alpha Ryker says.

My breathing finally slows down. My watch reads 8:45 pm. *In fifteen minutes, I can go home. Hopefully, Dad will be asleep from drinking too much.* I go back inside and wash up all the cups, mugs, and plates. The men leave the diner, and I breathe relief as I hear all of their car doors slamming. My body relaxes, knowing they have gone. Thinking Jim was behind me, I was just about to tell him I was leaving as well, but it wasn't Jim standing behind me. It's Ryker.

I avoid making eye contact with him. I'm aware my hood could fall any moment, revealing the abuse I suffer. His breathing is very noticeable.

'I'm sorry, sir. My shift is over. Please see Jim,' I say if you need anything else. His arm suddenly barricades the space between me and my exit as he presses his palm against the wall. I jump back in fright.

'Remove your hood,' he demands. I shake my head.

'No. Jim! Jim!' I yell as I try to move backward. But instead, I'm pressed against the wall with nowhere else to go. Then, without warning, I'm trapped between his body and the brickwork in one swift movement. He leans over me before planting his hands on either side of the wall.

'Jim is busy saying goodbye to his pack members out front. He thinks I've already left,' Ryker whispers, twirling my long brown hair in his fingers. He inhales my scent.

'You smell so good. Even my wolf is struggling to stay calm,' he confesses.

'You, you, have a pet wolf?' I'm scared. Ryker laughs at my question.

'Are you frightened of me, Astrid?' He asks. I nod.

'Well, if you are what my senses tell me you are and a rogue, you should be afraid. I don't know if I could have a rogue as my mate, and my pack might not want one as their Luna,' he explains.

'I'm sorry, sir. I'm confused. I'm not sure what you mean. Rogues, Lunas and Mates. I promise I won't be a problem to you if you just let me go home. We will never see each other again,' I whimper.

'In a moment, Astrid,' he whispers, looking down at my face, hair, and figure, clumsily clothed in my work uniform.

'Please. I want to go home. Please let me go.' I beg.

'I will let you go if you are not my mate,' he says.

'I don't know what a mate is. It would help if you stopped being an arrogant, obnoxious human being. Please, just let me go,' I plead.

Unleashing an angry growl, he punches the wall above my head. I drop to the ground in fright.

'Do not insult me like that again. Ryker scolds, 'How dare you refer to me as a human being?' Hugging my knees, I tremble.

'Please, just let me go home....'

He takes a step back and pauses, staring at me. He is in deep reflection. Curiosity and a pensive expression consume his handsome face.

'Alpha Ryker! What is the meaning of this? Astrid, are you okay? Why is there a hole in *my* wall?' Jim shouts before helping me up off the ground. The pressure of his hand on my broken rib makes me shriek in pain.

'Astrid, you're hurt. Your ribs. Please tell me you are, okay?' Jim says, worried.

Ryker's face softens as his concern for me replaces any anger he previously felt toward me. He takes a step closer to me, sharply inhaling the surrounding air. I move behind Jim for protection. Ryker looks away. Distancing myself away from him has offended him somewhat. His fists are clenched by his side as though he contains something within himself he cannot control.

'Ryker! What did you do to her? She's just a young, innocent girl! Did you break her ribs?' Jim shouts.

'I didn't touch her, Jim. She called me an arrogant, obnoxious human being. I got angry and punched the wall,' Ryker explains.

'Well, she got most of that right,' Jim yells, 'because you are being an arrogant, obnoxious--' Ryker stops him.

'Jim. Point taken! I overstepped the mark, but *she* acts like she doesn't know what a mate is. She's pretending she doesn't know she is a rogue!'

'That's because she doesn't know!' Jim yells. Ryker gives Jim a confused look, then looks at me. I'm just as bewildered.

'Look. I don't know what game this is, but I don't want to do this anymore. Just let me go home, and neither of you will have to worry about seeing me again,' I yell.

'Astrid. I'm so sorry about Ryker. Please. You don't have to leave your job here at the diner. You know you're safer here than at home,' Jim explains.

'What do you mean by that?' Ryker asks.

'Mind your own business,' I snap. Ryker backs away with a scowl. He crosses his arms and tries to hide the hurt look on his face.

'I *was* safer here, Jim, but Ryker has an agenda against me. I don't know what his problem is. Thank you for being kind to me and employing me all this time, but I can't work here anymore.' I kiss him on the cheek goodbye. His eyes are teary. Ryker lets out a growl. I go over to the stool where my handbag is and swing it on my shoulder.

'You! I feel sorry for whoever you seek and refer to as your mate! To be with you would be a curse!' I shout. My words deeply hurt him. He couldn't even look at me.

Before I can storm off and leave, Ryker swiftly takes my wrist. He flings my hood off my head rashly, and with the sharp eye contact we make, He feels a magnetic rush of endorphins and dopamine sweep through him. My stomach lurches at the instant feeling of butterflies. Everything around Ryker vanishes. He and I are the only people that exist.

I'm so confused. I don't know what is happening right now. A subtle, strange feeling flows through my body. Ryker is now staring at me as if he lusts after me, even though he was intimidating only minutes ago. I'm mesmerised by his eyes. This feels almost like I'm in a trance. Ryker stares intently into my green eyes before his eyes change in colour.

'You're my mate,' he whispers, stepping closer to me. I unwillingly snap out of the magnetic, lustful trance.

'Stop. Don't you dare touch me,' I yell. Jim stands there with a shocked look on his face.

'Alpha, are you sure Astrid is your mate?' Jim asks in disbelief.

'She's a rogue. This did not just happen?' Ryker mumbles to himself, brushing his hand through his hair, stressed.

'You're right. Whatever you think is happening is not going to happen. We can agree on that,' I say. Ryker stares at me.

'Who did that to your face?' He asks calmly.

'Mind your own business and stay away from me,' I say, skirring the kitchen through the diner and running out the door.

CHAPTER 3

Chasing after me, I hear Ryker's footsteps crunching on the gravel. I run faster, but he matches my pace effortlessly. Eventually, when I am out of breath, and my broken ribs cannot take any more, I am left with no choice but to stop and face him.

'Why are you following me?' I demand to know.

'You're my mate, whether or not we like it. I *have* to follow you. It's my business to know who did that to your face,' he says, firmly but calmly.

'You didn't care about me when you slammed your fist into the wall above my head!' I yell.

'Astrid, please, I'm sorry. I would never have done that had I known you were telling the truth about not knowing you're not human. I would have been more civil.' He looks at the ground guiltily.

'You have lost it now! Not being human? What is that supposed to mean?'

'How old are you?' His tone has changed again.

'I'll be eighteen in two weeks.' I try to avoid his eyes.

'You won't meet your wolf till then. I've had my wolf for four years. But I want to show you what I mean if you allow me to,' he says politely.

My breathing is heavy. I'm trying to stay calm and avoid feeling more upset than I already am.

'Are you okay?' He sounds genuinely concerned about my welfare.

'I don't want a wolf for my birthday, and I don't want to meet your pet wolf or any wolf!' I try to walk off, but the pain is too great.

'You've met a werewolf before?' He says, surprised.

'A werewolf? What is wrong with you? There is no such thing as werewolves. I'm talking about wild wolves. When I was little, my mum and I saw a wolf in the woods. Something bad happened, and I've been afraid of wolves ever since. I can't even go near pet dogs, let alone wolves.

So if you've got a pet wolf, I'm not interested.' I try to walk past him again, to no avail, as he steps in front of me again.

'What happened to the wolf?' He is curious.

'You're not very good at minding your own business?' I scold.

'Not when it involves *my mate*.' His reply is quick.

'You just said I'm a rogue, and you wouldn't have a rogue as a mate. So why do you keep referring to me as your mate when you don't even want me?'

Ryker steps closer to me, and it's impossible not to make eye contact with him.

'You're so beautiful and… stubborn. All I want to do is lift you in my arms and carry you home.' He is heartfelt and genuine. 'I want you to join my pack. You won't be a rogue anymore. We can be together.' His tone has dropped an octave again. If I hear more sincerity from him, I will melt right into this footpath. He slowly reaches his hand out to take mine.

I rescind away from him.

'No,' I say.

'No?' Ryker says, dumbfounded.

'You're asking me to be your girlfriend when we only just met. Not only that, you were an absolute jerk to me earlier. So, you only want to be with me because you feel sorry for me. And you want me to join your cult? Pack? Or whatever you call it. And talk nonsense about werewolves and fairies?' I yell.

'That's not what I meant. And I never mentioned fairies. Come back to the diner with me, and I'll explain everything. Everything you need to know about us, how it all works and what to expect,' Ryker tries to persuade me.

'We're werewolves?' I ask him. He stands there and nods.

'So, you're telling me I'm cursed? I'm stuck with you as a *mate*, and we're *werewolves*?' Ryker flinches,

'You're not cursed, Astrid. It's a blessing from the Moon Goddess,' he explains.

'You know what? I don't want to hear anymore. This is all too much. I am too tired and sore and don't even like you.' He stiffened at my words. I run as fast as possible toward the trees, hoping to lose him.

'Wait!' He yells, giving chase.

I hide behind a tree, trying to catch my breath, and remain as quiet as possible.

'Astrid. I know you're here. I can smell your scent a mile away,' he yells.

I dig my fingers into the mud underneath me and apply it all over my face and clothes. Ryker isn't far away from me. I imagine him inhaling the surrounding air, trying to catch my scent. But, of course, the darkness I'm sitting in makes it easier to conceal myself.

The chase is over after covering myself in mud. I know I am safe with Ryker, scentless and directionless. The diner is on the street that I pass. I'm an hour late, and I pray Dad is out drunk or asleep. I open the front door slowly and cringe at every creaking sound. No lights are on. Hopefully, this means he is sleeping. I carefully pad upstairs and open my bedroom door. With my light on, I see Dad sitting on the end of my bed with a furious look.

'Dad. I'm sorry. I can explain.' He is angry.

'Not only did you come home late, but you've dragged mud through my house!' He yells. I try to shield myself with my arms from the blows to no avail. Within seconds, I fall unconscious.

Not an inch of my body does not ache. I've spent the whole day being as still as possible to let my body rest. My memory of last night when I arrived home is hazy. I know my dad beat me, but I can't remember it. By evening, I find enough strength to run a small bath and wash the mud from my skin. Completely covered in bruises, my body is proof of the worst abuse it has ever sustained. I hug my knees and cry over the confrontation with Ryker last night and the beating I got when I came home. *Dad will kill me if he finds out about Ryker or me not having a job.* I wash the dishes and make some meals in the kitchen as best I can in my condition. I place them in the fridge. Dad should find them quickly enough. Sometimes I think I won't survive the subsequent beating, but somehow, I always do. I return to my room and fall asleep within minutes.

I'm still in pain the next day but have improved a little. I get dressed, brush my long brown hair, and apply some makeup to hide the bruising on my face. Dad expects me to be at work, but I can't go back after what happened the other night. I decide to go into town, a forty-five-minute walk from home, to apply for a new job. Close to the diner, I notice the black Mercedes behind me. I'm not in the mood for this. I am going to confront the person in the car. They know I'm waiting for them.

The car stops beside me, and a rear window descends. A man with dark hair and dark eyes smiles kindly. He has a weird scar near his ear. Half his ear is missing. I can't see the driver, but the two guys in the back look around twenty years old.

'Why are you following me?' I ask.

'Pardon my rudeness, young lady. My name is Zenith. Every day I go to work this way. You are alone on the road. I'm just concerned someone might take advantage of you. I want to keep an eye out for you and ensure you're safe,' he explains.

'Right. The only thing that worries me out here is this car with you and the creepy people in it,' I say.

'You're an unappreciative one, now, aren't you?' He says sternly.

'Look, Zenith, if you don't mind. I've had a terrible week. I need to get into town, so I'd appreciate it if you would stop following me and just let me be.'

'What happened to your job at the diner?' Zenith asks.

'How do you know I worked there?'

'I've seen you in there when I drive past to work.'

'Right.' I turn to walk away.

'Wait, take this.' He hands me his business card.

I take it reading it, *Zenith Creations CEO*, accompanied by a contact number. I look at Zenith, confused.

'If you need a job, call me,' he says.

'Thanks, but I'm sure I'll be fine,' I say, handing the card back.

'No, keep it. Just in case. I'll see you around, Astrid.' He gives me a wink before his window ascends, shielding him from view.

'Hey!' I yell as he drives off. 'How did you know my... name?'

I stand there watching the car drive further and further away. The diner is up ahead. I don't want to walk past it, but there is no other road to take. The woods are the only other thing around. There are more cars at the diner than there usually would be.

Jazz Ford

CHAPTER 4

A few of the same men I served the other night are standing outside the diner. They're staring intently at me. One man nods, and another enters the diner. I quicken my pace, knowing Ryker might be with them. I am left unbothered for a while, and I think this will be a non-event before Ryker suddenly stands in front of me. *You've got to be kidding me. How did he get here so quick?* I step around him.

'Astrid,' he says. I keep walking, and Ryker keeps pace with me. 'Astrid.' he repeats himself. I keep my head down and keep walking. He grabs my wrist, and I feel a subtle sensation from his touch.

'Ryker! Let me go!' I yell.

'No. I looked for you all night when you ran off and all day yesterday and today. So, we are going to the diner to talk,' he says.

'There is nothing to talk about!' I say, trying to pull away.

Ryker grabs me by the waist and lifts me over his shoulder. I cry out in pain from the injuries I sustained. Ryker quickly puts me back down.

'What's wrong?' He asks.

'Nothing, just please don't touch me,' I say. Ryker pushes my hoodie down.

'Astrid. I need you to look at me, please,' he pleads. He can see bruises on my neck.

I look into his blue eyes, tears rolling down my cheeks. I feel so ashamed of myself.

'Oh, Astrid...' he says as he tries to wipe my tears from my cheek. I flinch and take a step back. I'm not used to his kindness at all.

'Astrid, I didn't mean to hurt you,' he says.

'I know,' I say, looking away.

'Can you please walk with me to the diner and let us talk?'

Not knowing what else to do, I nod, and we walk toward the diner.

I don't have a chance to open the door at the diner before one of Ryker's men opens it for us.

'Alpha,' he says, nodding. Ryker walks in while I come to a halt and hesitate.

'You worked here for almost a year, and now you're afraid to come in?' Ryker says.

'I'd prefer Jim didn't see me like this,' I explain. Ryker stares at me for a moment.

'I'll tell him to stay in the kitchen,' he suggests. I hug my arms, nod, and keep my head down.

I hear a commotion of pots and pans falling a few moments later and Jim yelling, 'Let me see her, damn it.' Ryker is trying to hold Jim back. He is furious and distraught that my dad has hurt me again, this time worse.

I know Jim will not calm down anytime soon. I take a deep breath and go in.

'Jim, I don't want you to see me like this. I've caused quite the commotion. I am so sorry,' I say, standing at the kitchen bench and looking at the mess of pots and pans on the floor. Jim stiffens at the sight of me. I'm glad my hoodie and jeans cover the extent of my beatings.

'Astrid...' Jim says, staring at me. Then, his eyes well up, he steps toward me, and I rescind. He frowns and looks away.

'I'll get you some ice,' he whispers, walking to the freezer. The other men in the diner stare at me, sympathising with my injuries.

I make it obvious I'm uncomfortable by glaring at them. They all look away.

'Astrid, take a seat,' Ryker says, walking to the diner door, flipping the OPEN sign, and locking the door with the key. I am worried.

'It's fine, Astrid. We don't want to be interrupted. I'll unlock the door when you're ready to leave,' he reassures me. I nod and sit at the table with the booth seats. Ryker sits beside me. Jim passes me the ice pack and returns to the kitchen without looking at me.

'Astrid, we need to discuss your living arrangements,' he says.

'There's nothing to discuss,' I reply.

'Astrid, do you want him to kill you? Because looking at you in your current state, another beating before your eighteenth birthday, you probably won't survive,' he observes.

'Why would I not be able to survive another beating?' I ask. All the men in the room are listening to our conversation intently.

'She doesn't know about us or believe me. Yet,' Ryker says. The men speak with knowing looks, and unspoken words pass between them via their body language. I'm not privy to their thoughts.

Jim has made me a flat white coffee and some sandwiches. I'm so hungry. I eat slowly and carefully. The pain in my jaw makes it almost impossible, so I haven't eaten in days.

'Astrid, I'm going to explain everything to you, and I know you won't believe me yet, but you need to know now, so you know what to expect on your birthday. No matter what I say, try to stay calm. It's a lot to take in. The world you know is about to change,' Ryker says carefully, forming his words.

Too sore and too tired to argue, I keep sipping my coffee and listening.

'I live in what is called a pack. Every pack has an Alpha and a Luna, the pack's leaders. You are a rogue if you're not in a pack.' I raise my brow and tilt my head.

'So, I'm a rogue because I'm not in a pack?' I ask.

'Yes, that's correct. But being a rogue isn't a good thing. It makes you weaker. And you can't just go anywhere: you need permission to enter a pack's territory. Otherwise, they can punish you by instant death by a pack member in that territory,' he explains.

'That's not very nice to kill someone for passing through,' I say.

'Well, rogues are a threat and don't normally have good intentions for entering other territories. That's why,' he explains.

'Okay.'

'When you turn eighteen, something extraordinary happens to us. Our inner wolf wakes. You will hear your wolf in your mind. You'll also be able to heal quickly, and you will be able to shift into your wolf for the first time that night.' I laugh and see everyone looking very serious. They're all serious about this. This is no lie.

My attention turns to Jim. He places his hand over mine and gently squeezes it.

'Astrid, I know this sounds like some kind of fairy tale to you, but Alpha Ryker is telling you the truth, and you know I would never lie to you,' Jim says in a serious tone.

Pulling my hand away, I stand up. Ryker and Jim stand, too. I look around the diner again at all the men with serious expressions.

'I don't believe you. Either of you,' I say.

'Jim, would you like to do the honours and show her?' Ryker asks. Jim nods and starts undressing. I'm disturbed that Jim is stripping his clothes off right before me. I close my eyes and turn away.

'Jim! What are you doing?' I ask him. I hear sounds of muscles tearing and bones breaking. They're awful sounds. I've enlivened again with the chemistry between Ryker and me when he gently pulls my hands down from my face, forcing me to watch. After no time, Jim's face and body are covered in fur. He has morphed into a large brown wolf. I hyperventilate and go into shock from what I have witnessed.

The wolf howls and walks toward me. My ongoing screams force it to stop in its tracks.

'Wolf! Wolf! Wolf!' I cry and throw random objects at Jim. Anything I can get my hands on, the napkin holder, the salt, the pepper, the sugar, my empty mug, the jar of teaspoons from the table. I try to maintain a safe distance from him, but no space is safe when you're trapped in a diner with a wolf.

'It's okay, Astrid. Take some deep breaths. I know this is a shock for you, but you need to breathe. It's just Jim, and he will not hurt you.'

I sink to the ground in the corner and hold my knees as I tremble in fear.

'Ryker, please don't let it near me,' I say. The giant wolf whimpers and backs away into the kitchen, out of my sight. Ryker sits on the ground next to me.

'I told you I never wanted to see a wolf again! Why did you do that? Why do you want me to relive my mother's death?' I yell, slamming my hands repeatedly into his chest before letting myself slump forward. He wraps his muscular arms around me and holds me tightly. I'm instantly comforted by him and feel much calmer. His scent and his closeness console me. I suddenly feel very safe.

'I'm so sorry. I didn't know your mum died the day you saw the wolf. Please forgive me?' he whispers into my hair as he runs his fingers through it.

I'm furious with him, but I desire him. His arms around me make me feel the comfort I thought I'd never feel. I never want to leave his arms. It takes me a while, sitting in silence, to digest Jim shifting into a wolf and recover from my mum's death flashbacks.

Jim reappears in the dining room in his clothes, looking at me with a sad expression. I'm too scared to make eye contact or even look at him. He keeps his distance. A whole hour passes, with the memory of my mother's death replaying in my mind. Scenes from that day resound in my head, and poor Ryker does not know what I'm reliving as he holds me close. No one dares make a sound or move. The only noises I hear are the birds chirping outside and a few random, intermittent knocks on the diner's glass door because the diner is closed. Finally, I fall asleep in Ryker's arms.

CHAPTER 5

I look up to see Ryker staring down into my eyes with sadness.

'There's more I need to explain to you, but it can wait till tomorrow,' he whispers. I nod and look at the clock. *It's late! My father will kill me. I should have been home ages ago!*

Pushing myself out of Ryker's arms, I bolt for the door to leave, impatiently turning the handle clockwise and counter-clockwise to no avail.

'Where's the key?' I ask.

'Astrid! You're not going anywhere yet, and you aren't going back to that house!' Ryker argues.

'Ryker, you said you would unlock the door when I'm ready to leave! Please, you have to let me go. He will kill me if I'm late home,' I explain, trying to force the door open.

'Astrid, I won't let him lay a finger on you again. Do you hear me?' Ryker says sternly.

'He will hunt me down, Ryker. If I don't go home, he will kill me. He will look for me here,' I argue.

'Good. Let your dad come. Because it's the last time he will ever see you,' Ryker says.

'What are you going to do to him? You can't. You can't kill him,' I say.

'Why not? You will never have to fear him again if I kill him now.'

'I know he has hurt me, Ryker, but my mother loved him. She died because of me. I don't want to be the reason the man she loved dies too!' I cry.

Ryker steadies my chin with his hand to make me look at him.

'I think you should tell me what happened that day, the day your mother died,' he says.

'The only person I told is Dad. I don't want to do it again.' I look away in shame.

'Maybe in time, you'll tell me.' I give him a slight nod.

The phone at the diner rings. We look at each other, knowing it's my dad asking why I'm not home yet. Ryker nods to Jim to answer it.

'Yes, this is Jim's Diner. How may I help you?' Jim says.

'Yes, Astrid is here. But, no, she won't be coming to the phone. And no, she won't be coming home,' he says. 'Let me repeat myself. I don't think you got the message clear enough. Astrid is not coming back to your house again.' And after a few moments of Jim just listening, 'oh really? After what you've done to Astrid, my friends and I look forward to your arrival.' He slams the phone down and looks at Ryker. I look away. I don't know how to feel. My feelings are mixed. I feel happy and safe knowing Jim just stood up against Dad for me. Nobody has ever stood up against Dad for me. The feeling is liberating and daunting.

'He says he is on his way with his shotgun to come and take her home.' I freeze at his words.

'Ryker, I don't want anyone to get hurt. Just let me go back with him,' I whisper.

'No. If you go with your dad, it will never end. I don't want you to get hurt again. Or worse, killed,' he says.

'What happens to me isn't your problem, Ryker. I can look after myself,' I say. Ryker lets out an angry growl.

'It *is* my problem because you're *my mate*!' He shouts. We glare at each other for a moment.

'I know you're going to tell me tomorrow, but I want to know what a mate is right now because there is more to it than just being your *girlfriend*,' I say. Ryker sighs.

'Promise you won't freak out.'

'I'm not promising anything, Ryker.'

'Maybe we should wait till tomorrow, then. You have enough on your mind to process at this stage,' Ryker says. I slam my fist on the table.

'I want you to tell me now, Ryker!' I yell as I sit down on the chair opposite him.

Ryker looks away before inhaling and exhaling sharply. He sits down on the chair and looks into my eyes. His eyes convey a thousand untold stories. Maybe Ryker doesn't know where to begin. He stretches his arms out and opens his hands.

'Give me your hands,' he says with a soft smile.

'Why?'

'It will make it easier for me to explain what a mate is and the mate bond,' he says.

'Okay...' I whisper as I place my hands in his. Subtle sparks of electricity ignite in our skin. It gives me a warm, fuzzy feeling. He holds my hands and gently massages their backs with his thumbs, shooting electricity through my body.

'On our eighteenth birthday, when our wolf awakens, we can sense our mate when they're near. Sometimes we find our mates straight away and sometimes it takes years. Your mate will have the most amazing scent you've ever smelled. It will trigger your wolf in ways you can't hide, deny, or contain. Your wolf will want to follow the scent. Once you make eye contact with your mate, your wolf will announce that person is your mate. We develop an instant connection: it feels like magic and fireworks exploding when we touch each other. A need to be near each other at all times develops along with a sense of great desire for each other. We accept each other as mates by marking each other on the neck with our fangs. We bite each other, leaving our marks to show others we are mates. The bond intensifies. We can feel each other's emotions and sense each other at all times. Your mate is your life partner, your soulmate, the one you will spend the rest of your life with and have pups with. It's recommended to consummate the mateship as soon as possible to avoid attracting all the unmated males in the area who will want to mate with you. Oh, and I'm the Alpha, and you're my mate, so that makes you the Luna of the pack,' Ryker finishes. My reaction unsettles him.

I feel like a stunned deer in headlights. My mouth is agape, and I'm staring straight at Ryker. My mind goes into shock, registering all this new information. Then, slowly, I stand, inhaling and exhaling. I look at the back door through the kitchen. I'm as calm and as quiet as a mouse.

'Astrid? I--' he starts. I raise my index finger for him to be quiet. This is met with his confusion and a raised brow. All eyes are on me as I calmly walk toward the kitchen. I run like the wind as soon as I get to the back door.

He wants to bite me. Have sex with me. Make me carry his babies. Be his Luna. And stay with him forever? I only met him two days ago. This is not happening. They have all gone crazy! Or is it me going crazy? I don't even know anymore. If he thinks I'm going back home with him to be his lifelong mistress, he has another thing coming.

All these thoughts and questions envelop my mind as the pack chase after me. I run as fast as I can through the trees in the woods. But I don't get very far before being grabbed and pushed onto the ground by Ryker's quick arms.

He is as gentle as possible, but I'm in much pain from the beatings. Ryker lets out a slight growl.

'Why did you do that? Why did you run from me?' He asks.

'If you think for one second, I'm going back home with you to be your lifelong mistress and let you bite me and carry your pups. Maybe I'm better off back home, with my dad,' I say. Ryker flinches at my words.

'It's not like that at all. You'll understand it better when you turn eighteen,' Ryker explains.

'Get off me!' I yell. Ryker has me pinned to the ground on my back, and his face is an inch from mine. Our breath fogs as we pant in the cool night air.

'Will you run if I get off you?' He asks.

'Yes,' I mumble. Ryker lets out a low growl in displeasure. The sound of a shotgun goes off in the diner's direction. Ryker stands and takes my hand to pull me up. Our skin-on-skin contact is magical. I never want to let go of his hand.

As we return to the diner, holding hands, I fear what is about to unfold. My Dad is sitting on the bonnet of his car with his shotgun pointed at some of the pack members outside. He watches me step out from the concealment of the woods, holding Ryker's hand.

'How many men are here waiting to have their turn with you, Astrid? Fourteen? Fifteen?' He spits. Ryker lets out a growl.

'Astrid, you need to train your pet dog to behave. Otherwise, I'll have to put him down, like the dangerous dog he is for touching my daughter.' A warning shot fires toward Ryker's feet, purposely missing them but warning him. I jump at the gunshot. Ryker doesn't flinch. Instead, he maintains a steady resolve and holds my hand tighter. He glares at my father.

'The only one around here who needs to keep their hands off Astrid is you! I'm going to rip you to pieces,' Ryker yells, letting go of my hand and tackling my father to the ground. I try to grab his arms, but I'm useless. The scuffling is too unpredictable and quick for me to make any difference.

'No, please, Ryker. You can't kill him! Please!' I plead, my eyes well with tears. Ryker lets out a growl.

'I won't kill him. I'll just hurt him badly as he hurt you.' Ryker throws himself at my father. The shotgun goes off.

'No!' I yell. I go to help Ryker on the ground.

'Astrid, no. Stay back. Our pack will help him,' Jim says, holding me back.

'My Dad shot him, Jim! I need to see if he is okay.' I try to struggle out of Jim's hold, but it's no use: he is too strong.

My Dad is laughing. Ryker is still on the ground, and Dad thinks he is dead. Ryker moves, stands and throws himself at Dad. *Bang!* Another shot resounds in the night air. Ryker runs and tackles him off the bonnet onto the ground. Ryker snaps the shotgun in half, tosses it aside, and begins a succession of punches on Dad's face. I can see the blood escaping each time he hits him. Dad swings back at Ryker. Only a couple of attempts to make contact.

Dad tries to stand but is very unsteady. He falls over. With his arms pinned behind his back, Seth holds Dad up while Ryker punches him in the torso. Dad looks at me and grins while blood trickles from his mouth and nose. I can see gaps in his teeth where Ryker has knocked a few out. Ryker breaks Dad's ribs and beats him to near-death.

My Dad stares at me with a sick look, taking every hit like they're not affecting him, before speaking.

'This isn't the last time you'll see me, Astrid. You're the reason your mother is dead. I'll make you pay for killing her!'

Sick with emotion, I drop to the ground on my knees, unable to keep myself up. Dad laughs. With one look of sympathy for me from Ryker, he knocks him out cold.

Seth drops him, and he falls to the ground. Ryker is swaying, weak from all the fighting. He is drenched in sweat and blood and falls to his knees.

'I tried my best not to kill him,' he says deliriously.

'Ryker!' I yell. I rip his shirt open to find a bullet wound near his heart. I hold my hands over the bullet wound, putting pressure on it. There is blood all over my hands.

Jim, Seth, and the others gather around Ryker, shouting 'Alpha!' and 'can you hear me?' and 'quickly! Carry him into the diner. We have light there, and we can see what we can do to help him.' I remove my hands from Ryker's chest while a few pack members lift him and carry him into the diner.

Seth pushes the condiments off the table, clearing it, and the others place Ryker on the table. Blood is everywhere. I'm shaking with shock.

'He's going to be okay, isn't he?' I ask, distressed. Everyone turns and looks at me.

'We will try our best to save him, Luna. We need to remove the bullet so he can heal,' Seth explains. Jim returns to the table and gives Seth a knife, towels and other tools.

'Astrid, maybe you shouldn't watch. I can sit with you here,' Jim offers.

I hesitantly sit with Jim away from him, not wanting to leave Ryker's side. Jim puts his arm over my shoulder, pulling me into him. I'm shaking from all the trauma and sobbing.

'Luna, we removed the bullet. He should have healed by now, but nothing is happening,' Seth says, turning away as his eyes well up.

'No. Ryker can't die. Seth! I can't have someone die again because of me!' I say.

Pushing past Seth, I run to Ryker. The pack members move like I'm someone important. They give me some time with him. I lay my head on his chest and burst into tears.

'Ryker, please. I'm sorry. Please don't die. I'm sorry. It's all my fault. Please wake up.'

His breathing is faint. I sit up and put my hands over his wound. 'Please Ryker,' I cry. 'I promise I'll come home with you if you wake up.'

Placing my arms around Ryker, I return my head to his chest and cry. After a moment, warmth flows through my body.

'Astrid, none of this is your fault,' Ryker whispers as he caresses my back.

'Ryker,' I say, sitting up to look at him. The pack members race over to see Ryker waking up. I run my finger over the healed wound, now a scar. Ryker's eyes go completely black for a moment. 'It's healed!' I announce.

Ryker holds my hand and brings it to his lips, giving me a kiss that sends a hot shiver down my spine.

'It's because of you, Astrid. And our mate bond. I probably would have died if you weren't here,' he smiles.

'If I weren't here, Ryker, you never would have been shot.' I say.

Ryker pulls me into his chest and wraps his arms gently around me. Then, nuzzling his face into my neck, he sweetly whispers.

'It will take more than a bullet to take me away from you.' I want to melt into the floor at his words. But instead, I lean my forehead affectionately against his. Then, suddenly, I realise what I'm doing and push myself away from him, blushing. Ryker lets out a small chuckle.

'That is the mate bond,' he explains, smiling. I cross my arms and glare at him. Everyone laughs.

'You two make an interesting, cute couple,' Seth laughs.

'We aren't a couple,' I say. Ryker is more shocked than he should be.

It's awkward and quiet after that. Seth follows me out the front door, but I'm not planning on running. Instead, walking over to where Dad lies unconscious, I take in his blood-stained body. He is breathing but not going to be waking up soon.

Seth and I walk over to some grass and lie down to look at the stars and the moon. Ryker has a glum look, and the diner is probably full of chatter about what I said.

'Seth, I'm sorry if I upset you, your Alpha, and the others,' I sincerely say. Seth sighs.

'We need to remember. All this is very new to you, Luna. You haven't turned eighteen yet. I think once you've settled into Shadow Crest and adjusted to the way we werewolves live, everything will settle down for you,'

'This isn't the life I wanted. This isn't what I thought it would be, Seth,' I confess.

'That may be true, but it's a life that the Moon Goddess herself chose just for you, which is a great blessing, and an honour given to you,' he reassures me with a gentle smile. Ryker and the others come outside. Ryker puts his hand out to pull me up from the ground.

'How are you feeling?' I ask. Ryker smiles, 'Well, there's a hole in my heart. But it's alright because you came along and filled it,' Ryker says, referring to the bullet that struck close to his heart.

Pushing him away, I giggle. He smiles and opens the car door.

'Luna's in first,' he says. I roll my eyes and hop into the back seat with Ryker. We're sitting as close as possible.

'Are you trying to sit in my lap?' I joke.

'Can I?' He asks. We laugh.

'Let's get the hell out of here,' Ryker says. Seth drives toward Shadow Crest.

'How long does it take to get there?' I ask.

'Depends who's driving, I guess,' Ryker jokes. I give him a look.

'Okay, okay. Just under an hour,' Ryker answers. I yawn loudly against his chest.

'Sleep, my Luna, you need rest,' he whispers, holding me tightly as I drift off to sleep.

CHAPTER 6

It's around 1 am when we arrive at Shadow Crest. I wake up to Ryker carrying me in his arms. It's dark and quiet.

'Ryker, I can walk, you know?'

'I know, but I want to carry you,' he says with a grin.

'Put me down, Ryker.' He gently puts me down.

We are at the mansion's front entrance. It's three stories high. A giant white staircase ascends to the second floor. The balconies on the second and third floors are to die for, and I admire the white French doors and windows. Manicured green hedges border the mansion, and flowers grace the garden sweetly. A giant water fountain with two wolf statues is a glamourous outdoor focal point.

'This is where we live. This is the packhouse,' Ryker says proudly.

'It's a massive house for just two people,' I say.

'Oh, many of us live in this house.' Ryker scratches the back of his head nervously.

'You never said I'd be living in a house with a bunch of werewolves,' I say.

'It's normal for the Alpha and Luna to live in the packhouse with the beta, gamma, omega, and the cook. Guests from other packs come and visit too,' he explains.

'How can I stay with so many werewolves I don't even know?' I ask, crossing my arms.

'Astrid, no one here is going to harm you. On the contrary, you being here will bring a lot of excitement to Shadow Crest. I know it's a big change, but please give it a few days, and we will talk about it if you're still uncomfortable,' Ryker says.

Sighing, I say, 'Okay, fine.' Ryker opens the front door. Seth is behind us.

'Well, I'm going to jump into bed with my mate. I look forward to you meeting her after your rest Luna,' he smiles.

'I prefer Astrid for now,' I mumble. Seth and Ryker exchange their thoughts on what I ask of, with a hesitant look over my shoulder before he leaves and goes to his room.

'Come. Our room is on the top floor,' Ryker says as I follow him upstairs.

'Wait. Our room? Don't I get my own room for now?' Ryker pauses, and after a moment in thought, he nods.

'Your room, for now, will be the room beside mine.'

'Thank you,' I nod.

We make our way to the top floor. This place is immense. There are so many rooms and hallways.

'This is where I sleep,' Ryker says, opening a large door. It's an enormous room with a king-sized bed and walk-in wardrobes on either side. The windows are the largest I've ever seen in a house.

I look forward to seeing if the view during the day will be just as beautiful as the view at night.

'This way.' Ryker motions for me to follow him and steps into the room beside his.

'This room is your room. You have a walk-in wardrobe, a bathroom, a king-sized bed, a balcony, and a nice comfy couch in the corner here,' Ryker says. It's a beautiful room, only slightly smaller than his.

'Make yourself comfortable. This is your home now. There will be fresh towels in the bathroom when you wake up, and I'll ask Seth to see if his mate, Mia, can loan you something to wear. Then, when you're ready for breakfast, could you wait for me so we can go down together? Then I'll take you shopping for clothes, and you can meet some locals,' Ryker smiles.

'Okay, thank you,' I say appreciatively.

'Before I go. You've been through a lot tonight. Will you be okay on your own? I know you aren't comfortable sharing a bed just yet, but I can sleep on the couch here if you want me to?' I think about it for a moment.

'I think I'll be okay, Ryker.' He nods and leaves, closing the door behind him. I let out a yawn and walk over to the bed. It's so fancy and pretty and looks expensive. I eye the couch for a moment, curl up on it with a blanket, and fall asleep within minutes.

I look at the clock on the wall. It's just after 7 am. I sit up, rub my eyes, remembering everything from the night before, and look around the room as I realise *everything that happened last night wasn't a dream.*

I open the bathroom door. It's just as glamorous as the bedroom: the marble sink and the granite floor, the gold taps, and its chicness. In a cupboard, I run a bath and find many soaps, bubble baths, and lotions. *All these beauty products are every girl's dream.* Taking one of the bubble baths, I squirt it into the bathwater and place a body wash and shampoo on the side of the bathtub. Finally, I remove my dirty hoodie and jeans. I'm just about to discard my bra when there's a knock at the door.

'Who is it?' I ask.

'Hello, Luna. It's me. Mia! Alpha Ryker said you need something to wear. So I brought you one of my dresses. It will be warm today,' she says loudly and excitedly.

'Okay. Let me unlock the door.' I open the door to see a very sweet-faced, blue-eyed girl with brown, shoulder-length hair, around my height and only a little older than me. I'm guessing no older than nineteen. Her face lights up with the biggest smile before it changes into a look of horror.

'Luna! What happened to you? There are bruises everywhere!' She says, dropping the dress and covering her mouth with her hands in shock. I look down at all the bruising as I stand in my black underwear and bra. Then, ashamed, I hug myself and look away.

'Mia, just leave the dress and go, please,' I say.

'But Luna!' She says before I shut the door and lean against it so nobody can enter. 'Just leave the dress there, and go, Mia!' I say, wanting her to leave.

The bath is about to overflow. I run to it and twist the taps off. Then, removing my undergarments, I toss my underwear and bra on the floor and lower myself into the water. My whole-body stings while I scrub my body, wash my arms and legs and shampoo my long brown hair.

After the bath, I dry myself off. I find a neatly folded, maroon-coloured dress with a bra, some underwear and slip-on shoes. The short-sleeved dress sits just above my knee, hiding some bruises. The sweetheart neckline, unfortunately, doesn't hide much.

I find a brush behind the mirror door and see my reflection: my green eyes, small nose, and full pink lips. The bruising around my eye has faded a lot, thankfully. I apply a bit of foundation I find to hide what remains of the bruising.

Ryker and Seth are talking just outside my room.

'You know this will not go down well with Alice,' Seth says.

'I know, but I have my mate now, so things have changed.' I open the door. They go silent and smile at me.

'Luna, that dress is very flattering on you,' Seth smiles.

'Thank you,' I smile. Ryker walks over to me.

'You look beautiful, Astrid,' Ryker says. His face lights up with a big smile.

'I'm so hungry,' I announce.

'Well, you're about to meet Alice downstairs. She's the cook,' Ryker says.

Ryker insists on holding my hand down the stairs in case I fall. I know it's because he wants to be close to me and enjoys our closeness, just as I do.

We enter the dining room. A plate smashes to the ground.

'What is the meaning of this?' The older lady asks, staring at our hands.

Everyone stands at the table as we walk in.

'Alice,' Mia says, 'the special guest I was telling you about is our Luna. Can you believe Ryker finally found his fated mate?' Mia says in a bubbly and chirpy tone. Alice looks at me and glares.

'Now that you've met Astrid, your Luna, you can now finish serving breakfast,' Ryker says, smiling at me. Alice huffs off back to the kitchen. *What's her problem?*

Taking my seat at the table, Ryker sits next to me. Seth sits beside Mia and kisses her forehead.

'Astrid, you already know Seth and Mia. Over here are Gamma Kane and his mate Hayley.

'It's a pleasure to meet you,' Hayley says.

'Luna,' Kane says, bowing gentlemanly.

'Nice to meet you. Is Alice always this grumpy?' I ask. Everyone laughs.

'Actually, yeah. Alice can be full-on but ignore her.' Hayley smiles.

'Oh, okay.' I reply.

Alice comes out from the kitchen carrying a stack of pancakes while glaring at Ryker and plopping them down onto the table. Ryker follows her into the kitchen.

'Excuse me, Astrid, I need to get some water.' Moments later, we hear them arguing.

'Is everything okay?' I ask. Everyone passes, knowing looks across the table.

'I'm sure everything is fine, Luna,' Hayley says, reassuring me.

'So, you'll be eighteen soon?' Mia says.

'Yes, in nine days,' I smile.

'How exciting! It must excite you to meet your wolf?' She asks.

Ryker said something about shifting into a wolf on my eighteenth. I'm going to turn into a wolf. I don't want to shift and don't want to meet my wolf. What if I hurt someone or kill again? I can't repeat what happened to mum.

My chest suddenly feels heavy. I hyperventilate.

'Luna, are you okay?' Mia and Hayley ask. With teary eyes, I stand.

'I'm sorry. I can't do this! I can't be here!' abruptly, standing up, I run out of the dining room and down the hall until I find the front door and run down the street and keep running, with no idea where I am going.

CHAPTER 7

It's a beautiful town with lush trees and plenty of parks. I see a shopping strip and some cute cafes and clothing stores. There are plenty of people around who are most likely werewolves. I feel many unwelcome eyes on me. I perk up when I spot the watchtower and go there.

After climbing hundreds of steps, I take in the view of *Shadow Crest sure is beautiful.* A dense, green forest surrounds the town for miles, and I'm unsure which way to go. Finally, I sit down, defeated, and dangle my legs over the ledge, resting my head on the rail. *What am I going to do? Turning into a werewolf scares me, but I can't run from that. It's going to happen no matter where I go.* I reflect on last night: My dad shot Ryker, and he protected me from my father, and how my heart ached at almost losing him.

Suddenly, I feel a presence behind me. Ryker lets out a heavy sigh and sits down next to me, dangling his legs over the ledge.

'Ryker, I'm sorry I ran off. I panicked and didn't know what to do.' I explain.

'Do you want to talk about it? Mia mentioned what she said,' he says.

'How am I supposed to come to terms with shifting into a wolf, shifting into something I've always feared since I was seven years old? I don't want to meet my wolf, Ryker. I don't want to shift,' I cry. Ryker places his arm around me and pulls me close. His nose nuzzles my neck and sends tingles through my body.

'Astrid, I want to help you conquer your fears. On your first shift, I will be by your side. I will help you transition through it. I won't lie, the first time is the worst, but it gets easier. I promise to help you through it,' he says, tucking my hair behind my ear.

I nod and rest my head on his shoulder, silently taking in the view of Shadow Crest.

'If you're ready, we can go to the shopping strip. I'd like you to meet some people.'

'Okay, let's go,' I smile.

'Let's try Medley's clothing store,' Ryker says. He opens the door and a bell chimes.

'Welcome to Medleys. How can I help you? Oh. Alpha Ryker,' the sales assistant says, bowing her head.

'What an honour to have you in my store. It's been a while,' she gives him a platonic, friendly wink.

'And who do we have here?' She smiles while looking me up and down.

'Astrid, I'd like you to meet Medley. She is the owner here and will help you pick out some clothes,' he says smiling, 'and Medley, this is your Luna, Astrid,' he tells Medley.

Medley's jaw drops on *Luna,* and she bows her head.

'I'm sorry. I did not know Alpha had found his mate. How did Alice and Vanessa react to the news?' She asks. Ryker looks at me, then back at Medley.

'Alice found out this morning, so she will probably inform Vanessa that the agreement is no longer happening today.'

'Right. Well then, Luna, if you'd like to come this way, with me, into the change rooms, and we'll try on some clothes,' she says.

Following Medley, I ask Ryker, 'who is Vanessa'?

'She is just a friend who has always had a crush on me, but I wouldn't worry yourself over it too much,' he says.

'Is that why Alice wasn't thrilled this morning?' I ask. Ryker nods.

'Yeah. Vanessa is her daughter, and all of Shadow Crest knows she wants to be my mate and Luna,' he explains.

'She doesn't have a mate?' I ask.

'Her mate died in her old pack, Shady Crest, two years ago. She transferred to our pack after he died. She says they were abusive toward her, forcing her to be the pack slave. Alice and Vanessa ran away and found themselves here, and she developed a silly crush on me,' he explains. I nod, accepting his explanation, and continue to the change room where Medley has hung dozens of dresses, tops and skirts for me to try on. In what feels like a fashion call in a movie, Medley shows me a consecutive offering of chic clothes in an assortment of fabrics.

'Do you have anything more casual?' I ask.

'You're a Luna and should dress as such,' she smiles.

'I haven't agreed to be anyone's Luna. I'd just like normal clothes like everyone else, please.'

'Surely Alpha has marked you?' She asks, looking at my neck. I grab her wrist before she moves my hair aside and sees the bruises.

'You will keep your hands to yourself!' I say sternly.

'Luna, forgive me. I'm so sorry. I'm completely out of line. It's unheard of not marking your mate right away, especially being an Alpha's mate.'

Medley excuses herself while I try on some clothes. I choose three casual dresses, a few pairs of jeans, a few tops, a couple of hoodies, and a couple of cardigans to go with the dresses. Medley returns with a few bra-and-underwear sets.

'These are the clothes I've chosen. You can take them to the counter with the undergarments you're holding,' I say.

Following Medley to the cash register, she scans the items and places them into shopping bags.

'Is there anything else you need, Astrid?' Ryker asks as he pulls his gold card out to pay.

'Maybe a nightie to sleep in, but I don't know if there are any in this store.'

'There are a few other clothing stores we can go to,' he says. I nod, and we leave the store. Ryker insists he carries the bags.

We pass the next couple of shops and go into a nightwear store full of pyjamas and nighties.

'Alpha, it's a pleasure to have you here. What do I owe the pleasure?' The sales assistant says before looking at me.

'Daisy, this is Astrid, my mate. Astrid, this is Daisy,' he says.

'Oh! We finally have a Luna! The elders must be so thrilled! And you, of course, Alpha!' She walks over to me and hugs me. I flinch as she squeezes me. Then, I cry out in pain.

'Astrid, are you okay?' Daisy asks, stepping back with worry.

'I'm okay. My ribs are still healing, is all,' I say.

'I should take you to see the pack doctor to ease the pain,' Ryker says.

'It's fine, as long as I don't get squeezed again,' I say.

'Luna, I am so sorry! Whatever happened to you?' She asks.

'It's fine, Daisy. You didn't know. I fell down some stairs at home,' I lie, looking away.

'Anyway, we're here because Astrid needs some nightwear,' Ryker says, changing the subject for me.

Before we enter the change room, I give Daisy different pyjamas sets. I find some of the silliest items I have no intention of buying. I put on a green dinosaur onesie with a long tail and exit the dressing room. The hood is the shape of a dinosaur's face. Ryker bursts out laughing.

'What about this one?' I ask. Ryker is still laughing.

'If that's what you want to sleep in, be my guest,' he says. I return to the change room, giggling, before trying on an astronaut onesie. I walk out in slow motion as though I'm on the moon.

'Houston, we have a problem,' I say. Ryker laughs again.

'What's the problem?' He asks, chuckling.

'The zip is stuck!' I say, strolling back into the change room.

Ryker follows me into the small change room he can barely fit in and closes the door behind us. He runs his finger down my spine to find the zip, eliciting a small moan from me. He let outs a slight cheerful growl while slowly unzipping the back of my onesie. I turn to face him.

Our faces are almost touching. It is sweltering in the change room.

With eyes transfixed on each other. Our breathing becomes heavy. I close my eyes, relishing Ryker's warm touch on my face. When Daisy opens the door, we're pressed closely to each other, and our lips are about to meet.

'How are you going in there? Oh, my goodness! I'm so sorry!' She says, blushing and turning around. Ryker and I straighten ourselves up.

'It's fine. Astrid is ready to try on the next one,' he says, with a grin and a cheeky wink. I blush, and Ryker exits the tiny cubicle.

'Here, please tell Astrid to try these on,' he tells Daisy. Daisy hands me a maroon two-piece set made from silk. The top is a button-up, short-sleeve silk shirt, and the bottoms are shorts. I think they're pleasant and modest when I try them on.

'These are comfy,' I say, walking out with a smile.

'Great. I'll buy that set of pyjamas for you. Maybe try this set on too,' he says, grinning. I turn before getting changed. Ryker and Daisy are giggling.

'Is there something wrong?' Daisy blushes and looks away.

'Nope, nothing's wrong,' Ryker says, smiling, his arms crossed.

Later, I discover the source of their amusement when I put them away: the silk set has *Bite Me* printed on the bum. The pants I try on are very soft and have a slight fluffiness. I can alternate between a singlet top and a long-sleeved shirt with them. Finally, I walk out, only to laugh. Ryker wears the same dark-blue set in the male set.

'I thought we could have a matching set,' he laughs.

'Fine,' I smirk, shaking my head in disbelief. I change back into my clothes. Ryker has changed and has paid for everything.

'Want to look around the other shops?' Ryker asks.

'No, I think we're ready now.'

'Okay, let's go.'

We get back to the packhouse in ten minutes. No one else seems to be around, so we go upstairs to put my clothes away. Ryker lies on his back with his eyes closed. I lean on the bedpost, admiring his handsome face for a few moments before lying beside him.

'Astrid?' Ryker spoke.

'Mmhmm?'

'I'd like you to meet my wolf tonight. He looked at me and said, 'I want to remove your fear of us.' I turn on my side.

'Okay, but I only want to meet yours for now,' I reply.

'Okay,' he kisses me on the forehead.

Jazz Ford

CHAPTER 8

We decide to watch some movies downstairs.

'Can we make some popcorn first?' I ask.

'Sure, I'll make it while you pick a movie.' I flick through the list. There are so many to choose from that I can't decide. I close my eyes and press play on a random movie. Ryker sits beside me, holding a large bowl of salty, buttery popcorn.

'What are we watching?' He asks.

'I'm not sure. I couldn't decide, so I closed my eyes and picked a random movie.'

'That's cute,' he smiles. I giggle. Then, the movie starts and happens to be a scary horror film. I have my face in Ryker's shoulder halfway through it, too frightened to watch the spooky parts anymore.

'You can hold my hand if you're scared,' he says. I laugh.

'You wish!' I laugh.

'I wish,' he says, grinning. I smile back at his confidence and jump in fright when the monster appears on the screen, out of nowhere, capturing and killing the human who tried to get away.

'Aww, baby. Did the monster scare you?' Ryker asks as he swings my legs over his to cuddle me like a baby. I swat him, laughing, and lay my head on his chest.

'Shh, I can't hear the movie,' I whisper. Ryker laughs.

I don't feel so afraid watching the movie in Ryker's arms anymore. Seth, Mia, Kane and Hayley arrive home just before the credits. They smile when they see me in Ryker's lap. When the movie finishes, I get up and go over to the others.

'I'm sorry about running away this morning, guys. I didn't mean to upset anyone.'

'It's fine, Luna. We didn't realise how new you are to all this. Seth filled us in. We felt so bad for upsetting you,' Mia says. We exchange little smiles, and I hug Mia.

'Ryker and I are going to watch another movie. You should join us,' I tell them.

'Sure,' Hayley says.

'Yep, sounds good!' Mia says. The boys follow suit, making themselves comfortable. Ryker smiles and pats his lap. He is happy we're watching another movie, so I snuggle into him. I can't refuse the offer if I try. His powerful arms and masculine chest are a very comfortable place to be. The girls can't decide on a movie, so I take the remote from Mia before pressing play on something random again. Of course, it's another horror film, to the boys' delight. We girls are not great with horror films. We keep screaming, jumping, and flinching. Having our mates holding us closer makes it all worth it.

After the movie, right at dinner time, Alice still has a scowl on her face and tries to avoid me as much as she can. Ryker takes my hand and leads me outside, where we wander through the garden in the dark.

'Sit here and close your eyes for me,' he says. I sit down with my legs crossed and my eyes closed.

'What are you doing?' I ask.

'I'm going to change into my wolf form. You can keep your eyes closed while you pat me, okay?' Suddenly, I'm nervous, but I nod and close my eyes, trusting him. A moment later, Ryker, in his wolf form, nuzzles his fury face into my hands affectionately. My hands are shaking. Tears roll down my cheeks. Flashbacks of my mother dying keep appearing in my mind. He whimpers to assure me it's okay. I'm too scared to open my eyes, but his fur is soft. I cautiously raise my hand and place it on his smooth, furry face. He is panting happily like a dog, and his tail dusts the ground in excitement. I let the fur glide between my fingers. I have both hands on the sides of his face. He steps closer and rubs his wet nose on my cheek. I giggle.

'It tickles!' I laugh. I put my arms around his neck, and he rests his head on my shoulder. I rub my face in his fur. It's so soft and warm.

'I think I'll try to open my eyes. I want to see what you look like,' I say. Ryker sits down in front of me, waiting obediently. I slowly open my eyes, letting the moonlight adjust my eyesight. Exhaling in awe, he is the most impressive wolf I have ever seen: his coat is long, black, and sleek. It shines and glistens in the moonlight. There is a sense of greatness and power emitting from him. His four-pawed stance is one of pride. He nudges my face with his muzzle. I hold his face close to mine, enjoying the warmth and the connection.

'Thank you, Ryker,' I say, tears rolling down my cheek. He whimpers and licks my cheek.

'Ryker! That's so gross!' I laugh and push him back. I stand and run, and he happily chases me. As I run through the trees, my long brown hair blows in the wind behind me. I zigzag through the trees with Ryker, and his tail wags like a puppy's. After a while, I sit down to catch my breath. He nudges my shoulder and gives my cheek another lick. I giggle and push him away with my hand — Ryker motions to his back.

'You want me to hop on your back?' I ask. He nods.

He has to lie down so I can climb onto his back because he is so tall. Once I'm on his back, I grip onto his fur, and he runs further into the woods. He runs at great speed—adrenaline courses through my body. The breeze whips past my face, and I can't help but smile. The feeling is exhilarating. I hold my arms out and bask in the wind rushing past us.

Something out the corner of my eye catches my attention and races toward us.

'Ryker, there's something—' Before I can finish my sentence, someone has forcibly knocked me down from Ryker's back. I roll across the ground and plunge into a tree.

Growling and teeth-baring ensue in a fight. There is a rugged, small, brown wolf with a grey patch snapping at Ryker from where I lie. I try to stand, but everything is spinning. I remain where I am against the trunk of the tree.

Ryker and the other wolf encircle each other, snapping and growling in a stand-off. Ryker uses his Alpha telepathy and orders her to shift. They both change into their human forms. Ryker and the female wolf shift into human form. He is entirely naked with his back to me. A young woman stands facing Ryker. She is beautiful and has long, blonde hair, brown eyes, a good sized-bust and a curvy, toned figure.

Letting out a growl, I glare. She glares back at me and crosses her arms. *Did I growl like a wolf?*

'Vanessa! You just hurt your Luna!' Ryker yells.

'*I* am *your* Luna!' She snaps.

'Vanessa, we will discuss this another time. First, I need to see if Astrid is okay,' he says as he walks over to me. My vision is blurry. My head hurts. I realise I must have bumped my head on the tree trunk. Ryker grabs my arms to pull me up. He asks, 'Are you okay?'

'I think I hit my head. Everything is spinning,' I say, rubbing my head with one hand and leaning onto Ryker. Vanessa marches toward us.

'Don't you walk away from me, Ryker!' She yells.

'Go home, Vanessa! We will discuss this tomorrow!' He yells back.

'I love you, Ryker! I know you love me too. We have already made the arrangements. I'm your mate and Luna!' She yells. Gasping at her words, I look up at Ryker.

'Is this true, Ryker?' I ask, praying that it isn't. Ryker lets out a sigh.

'Yes, it's true, but—' I slap Ryker across the face before he can finish his sentence.

'You made me come here. You convinced me to give you a chance, and you already had a mate and Luna?' I yell. Ryker has his hand on his cheek, where I slapped him.

'Astrid, you don't understand. I can explain all this. You are my true mate, my fated mate. Vanessa was just a chosen mate. It's not the same! I didn't want—'

'Enough!' I say sternly. I look at Vanessa standing behind Ryker, smirking.

'You can have him!' I yell, making her grin.

'Astrid, please hear me out. You don't understand!' Ryker says as he tries to take my hand. I back away from him.

'You know, I thought we had something special and magical until your whore arrived!' I yell. Vanessa glares at my words.

Turning, I run toward the house. Ryker wants to chase after me, but Vanessa grabs his arm. I see Vanessa trying to hug Ryker, but Ryker is yelling at her and pushing her off him.

'I love you, Ryker!'

'The feeling isn't mutual,' he growls.

I shove the front door to the packhouse open. Everyone inside the packhouse rushes toward me and asks if I'm okay.

'Why don't you all ask Vanessa?' I snap at them as I run upstairs and slam the door to my room closed. I curl up on the same couch I slept on the night before.

I finally receive some happiness, only for someone else to come along and ruin everything. Why can't I have some consistent happiness in my life for a change? Will I ever know what it's like to be loved, to feel special and wanted?

CHAPTER 9

The following day, there is a knock on my locked door. I ignore it.

'Astrid, I know you're there. Please unlock the door,' Ryker pleads. I don't want to hear his voice, so I lock myself in the bathroom, run a bath, and stay there for as long as possible.

I put on a pair of jeans and the most oversized hoodie I could find. It almost touches my knees. I pull the hood over my head. It makes me feel invisible, like I'm able to hide from the world. It's an enormous sense of comfort.

On the twelfth knock on my door, Ryker is livid and enlists Mia's help.

'It's Mia, Astrid,' she says through the door. As sweet and bubbly as she is, I still want to be left alone.

'I brought you some lunch. I'll leave it at the door,' she explains.

The last thing I want to do is eat food. I feel sick thinking about how close I have become with Ryker. He wants me, but I don't understand why. *I know I'm his mate, but he had already arranged to be mates with Vanessa. Have I ever meant anything to him? Or has he been playing me and lying to me this whole time?*

Exiting the bathroom via two gorgeous French doors, I sit on the balcony next to a large pot plant, hoping no one can see me. I keep hearing the odd door-knock for the rest of the day and continue to ignore it. Sometimes it's Ryker knocking. Sometimes it's other people. It hurts me every time to hear the pain and regret in his voice when he speaks. Hayley knocks on the door when it's dinnertime.

'I brought you some dinner, Luna. I see your lunch is still here. I know you're upset, Astrid, and I understand why, but Ryker is so distressed we're struggling to keep him calm. We could use your help to calm him down before he destroys the entire house.'

Feeling a little guilty hearing that Ryker is tearing the place apart, I let out a heavy sigh, walked to the door, and unlocked it. Hayley is holding a plate of food and smiles at me.

'Luna. Thank you.'

'Thank you, Hayley. I'm not hungry. Can you show me where he is?' Hayley nods.

I follow her downstairs, where Ryker is growling and throwing a chair across the living room. The room is a complete mess. I stand there with my arms crossed, unimpressed with the absolute mess he has made. Ryker sniffs the air and spins around to see me. He races over to me, relieved. I look away, not wanting to look at him.

'Astrid! You've come out,' he says, kneeling before me, clutching my hands. Everyone is watching us. Ryker has been crying. He looks up at me with big puppy dog eyes, it's endearing, and I'm struggling to stay mad at him.

'Astrid, I never wanted Vanessa to be my mate or Luna. I'm twenty-two. The elders told me they would have to choose a mate for me because I hadn't found my fated mate yet,' he explains.

'Why didn't you tell me that before?' I ask.

'I tried, but you were upset and locked yourself in your room.' He is looking down at the ground. I kneel on the floor, facing him.

'I'm sorry. Had I known, I wouldn't have locked myself in my room. I'm feeling guilty.

'It's okay. You're out now. That's all that matters.' He smiles, holding my face and patting my cheeks with his thumbs.

'I spoke to Vanessa and told her the agreement was off. I never agreed to any of it. The elders put it all in place, even though I was against it. I know she has always had a crush on me, but I felt nothing for her,' he explains.

'Vanessa will adjust to it in time,' Hayley reassures me. I nod at Hayley.

'How's your head?' He asks, both of us standing up.

'My head feels fine now,' I say.

'Join us for dinner,' Ryker says.

'I'm exhausted. I'd rather sleep for the night,' I say.

'You haven't eaten all day, though. Eat, and then you can go to bed,' he says. I nod, and we sit at the table where Alice has placed assorted platters of food from which we can serve ourselves.

Sitting down at the table, Vanessa walks in, smiling. She sits down at the table and scoops food onto an empty plate. My fork hasn't even reached my mouth yet. I freeze with her presence, and everyone feels awkward.

'What is she doing here, eating dinner with us?' I ask Ryker.

'Don't you know? I live in this packhouse too,' Vanessa says with a sour look. My fork drops from my hand at her words and clutters noisily down onto my plate.

'You have got to be kidding me,' I say.

'When the elders arranged for her to be Luna, they expected her to live here,' Ryker explains.

'I'm here with Ryker now, Vanessa. You don't need to be here anymore,' I smile.

Mia smiles at my confidence, and Vanessa glares at her.

'I heard along the grapevine that you might not even want to become the Luna or accept Alpha Ryker as your mate,' she says. Ryker growls and glares at her. If looks could kill, his would.

'That's none of your business.' I snap at her.

'Well, it is my business because if you don't accept Alpha Ryker within a certain time frame, the elders will still make Alpha Ryker mark me as his mate and initiate me as the Luna of Shadow Crest,' she says happily.

I growl at her words. *Did I growl like a wolf again?* Everyone turns to stare at me, surprised at my reaction.

'Would they make you do that?' I ask him. Ryker thinks for a moment.

'There is a possibility, but I'm sure it won't come to that because you're here now. I don't see why we would have to rush anything,' Ryker says. Vanessa giggles.

'I guess we'll see what the elders prefer: your true mate who is weak and hasn't met her wolf yet and knows nothing about our world, or me: someone experienced and strong and willing to bear your pups straight away,' she smirks.

Ryker and I growl in unison at her words. I exhale sharply.

'You're nothing but a scruffy little dog from the woods!' I snap. Mia, Hayley, and Kane burst out laughing. Seth tries to keep his composure. Vanessa stands.

'How dare you! I came from one of the strongest packs in the world. Shady Crest! We are—' I cut her off.

'Shady,' I say. The entire table is roaring with laughter.

'At least I know what pack I come from,' she snaps.

Everyone goes silent, bracing themselves for my reaction.

'For all we know, you could be from one of the weakest packs: the Rabid Rebels or the Astral pack. I can assure you when we meet your wolf, we'll know, and if you're from a weaker pack, the elders will intervene. So you won't be allowed to rule as Luna. I'll be chosen in your place instead!'

'And what if I'm not? What if I'm from one of the strongest packs?' I snap.

'Well, the strongest pack used to be the Moonstone pack. They have pure white wolves, but they had been wiped out around eighteen years ago, so keep dreaming! Shady Crest is the strongest now, and our wolves are brown, and I have never seen you there. Shadow Crest comes next. Alphas are black, and pack members are grey,' Vanessa explains, smirking at me, feeling victorious.

'So, we already know you aren't from a powerful pack. So, until you're the official Luna, I'm still in the running,' she concludes.

'Actually, Vanessa. I think it would be best if you moved out of the packhouse tomorrow. Seth will organise one of the nearby cabins for you to remain close to your mother.'

'You can't be serious?' Vanessa yells.

'Yes, I'm very serious. You will move out tomorrow.'

'You can't kick me out, Ryker. You can't make me move out!'

'If you are not out by lunchtime tomorrow, I will drag you out of this packhouse myself,' Ryker growls.

Standing up from the table, I walk away.

'Astrid, where are you going? You haven't even touched your dinner,' Ryker growls.

'I lost my appetite. I will not stay here and listen to this scruffy little mutt anymore!' I storm off to my room and shut the door, locking it again.

If she thinks she can speak to me like that and treat me like that, she has another thing coming!

Jazz Ford

CHAPTER 10

Last night was awful. I wasn't able to get much sleep. I got up early before sunrise and headed downstairs to the kitchen to make myself breakfast. Entering, I freeze for a moment as Alice is there, cutting up fruit. Alice pauses and looks up to see me. She becomes angry and the knife in her handshakes.

'Good morning, Alice,' I say politely. She growls in a warning.

'I'm just going to get myself something to eat, and then I'll be gone,' I say.

'Permanently, I hope,' she mutters.

'Alice, I get you're upset, but I planned none of this. I didn't even know werewolves existed until recently. Maybe if we get to know each other, we might come to tolerate each other. Maybe even be friends,' I say. I yelp when her knife flies past my face and into the wall.

'I will never be your friend, and you will never be my Luna! Mark my word, Vanessa will become the Luna of Shadow Crest! So I suggest you save yourself from the hurt and leave now. Because I can assure you, you won't live to see your eighteenth birthday!' Alice warns.

'Did you just threaten to kill me?' I ask, in disbelief, looking at the knife in the wall. Alice closes in on me. I steel myself for whatever's next.

'If you're not gone from here by your eighteenth birthday, Vanessa and I will shift and rip you apart! And if you speak of this conversation to Alpha Ryker or anyone, I'll ensure it's the last day of your life!' She snaps. I'm trying to keep my emotions intact.

'Why do you hate me so much? Don't you want Vanessa to be happy? How could she be happy with a man who doesn't love her? A man who doesn't want to be with her?'

Alice grabs my hair and pushes me against the wall.

'Oh, Astrid, sometimes in life, it's not about love, but other things like power,' she says, retrieving her knife.

I'm scared and try to hide my fear.

'If I were you, Astrid, I'd get going right now, before everyone wakes up,' she says, tapping my nose with the knife. She stares at me and holds the blade against my face. I nod.

'Good! Well, it was nice meeting you, Astrid. I hope we don't cross paths again,' she smirks, and I leave the kitchen hysterical and affected.

She is going to kill me! She is going to kill me if I stay! I don't want to leave Ryker or the others. How can I tell them without her finding out?

Bursting into tears, I dress quickly in jeans and a hoodie. I grab a small pack and place another set of clothes in it. *Do I leave? Do I leave a note? Where will I go? I can't go back to my stepfather's house. Maybe I can camp in the woods for a few days. I can sneak food from the diner until I figure something out. The sun is rising. I have to leave now.*

I climb over the balcony and down the latticework beneath. I run opposite the shopping strip, hoping it leads me toward Jim's diner. A couple of hours pass me by when I'm deep in the woods, and I freeze at the faint howl of a wolf in the distance. I know it's Ryker, realising I'm gone. Falling to the ground, I cry.

'Please forgive me, Ryker. I didn't want to leave. I didn't want to leave you.'

Standing, I wipe my tears. They're uncontrollable. I suddenly remember when Ryker explained he could smell my scent. I look around and grab some eucalyptus leaves from a low-hanging branch. Removing my hoodie and jeans, I rub the leaves down my legs all over myself. I put my clothes back on, sticking a handful of eucalyptus leaves into my hoodie and jeans pockets. I run further into the woods. After a while, I resort to walking because I'm exhausted. *Ryker would have followed my scent until I used those leaves. I should probably change course, too, if he keeps going straight.*

Changing my direction, I stop at a riverbank to drink some water, hoping it's clean enough. The sun is setting. I have to find shelter soon before it becomes dark. I wander around until I find a large hollow log on its side.

This will be perfect. I crawl into the hollow log and open my bag, covering myself with the other jumper to keep as warm as possible. I sleep curled up and use my bag as a pillow. The sun rises, and I'm surprised I slept all night.

I've been walking for three hours. I'm happy when I see a familiar road. It leads *into the city!* I stay off the road to avoid Ryker finding me. The black Mercedes is in the distance. I sense it's a bad idea to run toward it, but I do.

Out on the road, I watch the black Mercedes slow down to a halt. The back window rolls down.

'Hello, Zenith,' I say.

'I was worrying, Astrid. I haven't seen you for a few days,' he says.

'I'd like to take you up on that job offer if you'll still have me?' I ask nervously. Zenith smirks.

'When can you start?' He asks.

'I can start now if you like?'

Zenith looks me up and down, studying me. He is curious.

'Has something happened, Astrid?' He asks.

'I'm no longer living with my father, and no one here is looking to employ new staff,' I explain, leaving Ryker out of the story.

'I see,' he says, scratching his half-missing ear. He opens the car door and gets out.

'You may as well hop in. You work for me now,' he smiles. I glance around to make sure no one is watching and climb into the car.

Zenith scans the area to see what I'm looking at and says nothing about it. A young guy in the car smiles at me and pats the seat next to him, motioning for me to sit. Sitting next to him, I click my belt.

'Astrid, this is John, one of my twin sons,' Zenith introduces him.

'Nice to meet you,' I say, politely holding my hand out to shake his. John places a kiss on my hand as he takes it.

'It's a pleasure to meet you, Astrid,' he replies with a cocky smile. He looks a lot like Zenith but less bulky and much thinner. He has the same dark eyes, dark hair, and nose. A few days of stubble have grown on his face.

'So, your business, *Zenith Creations:* what is it you do exactly?' I ask. Zenith chuckles.

'I do many things. Mainly, I have meetings with high-profile clients. I go through their designs and make their products,' he explains.

'Oh, okay. What are you employing me to do?' I ask.

'I need a personal assistant to take calls, book appointments, make coffee, and run little errands,' he says.

'Okay,' I smile. I look out the window, wishing *things were different with Ryker. I want to be in his arms and wish Vanessa and Alice weren't part of the pack.*

'Astrid, I need to talk to you about something before we arrive,' Zenith says. 'It's brilliant of you hiding your scent with those leaves. I suggest you leave them in your pocket until we arrive at the workplace.'

'How do you know I'm a werewolf?' I ask, surprised. Zenith's eyes change into his wolf's eyes.

'I'm also a werewolf and the Alpha of my pack.' His eyes change back to his human irises. John is grinning. My chest suddenly feels tight, and I hyperventilate.

'Stop the car, please!' I yell.

'Ignore her, Ralph. She is just overreacting,' Zenith says to the driver, placing his hand on my shoulder, making me cringe.

'Astrid, you are one of us. I will not hurt you. I'm hoping you'll even consider joining my pack. You'll have our full protection from whoever you're running from,' he smirks.

'I'm not running from anyone.'

Zenith sighs and pinches his brow bone with his thumb and index finger.

'Astrid, you don't have to play dumb. I know you're running from someone. Who are you running from?' He asks.

'It doesn't matter whom. I won't see him again,' I say sadly and look away.

'Well, my offer always stands, become part of my pack, and you'll always have full protection,' he repeats.

'We've arrived,' he says as the car stops. He opens the car door and reaches his arm out for my hand to help me out of the vehicle.

'Thank you,' I say, stepping out of the car and feeling John brush up behind me as he gets out of the vehicle. I step forward to put space between us and ignore him.

Jazz Ford

CHAPTER 11

We're in an underground car park. I follow Zenith to an elevator, step in and stand beside Zenith at the back. John stands in front of us. I feel under-dressed, wearing a hoodie and jeans while they wear expensive suits. After a few minutes, the elevator stops and the doors open with a *ding.* I step into a large, clean, classy foyer. I follow Zenith to a large door.

'This is the waiting room.' he says.

The waiting room has luxurious couches and recliners, designer coffee tables, fancy vases and fresh flowers. There is a long u-shaped desk centred in the room and an ample water feature on another wall.

'This will be your desk. You will greet the clients and offer them drinks. There is a kitchen with a coffee machine and a fridge behind you. Give my clients whatever they want,' he says. I nod.

'This room behind your desk is my office. Don't let anyone in until you have told me they are here via call. I will tell you when I'm ready for them.'

'What if they refuse to wait and enter your office?' I ask.

'Use your common sense, do what you must just don't let them in,' he says.

'Okay,' I say, exhaling and visualising all plausible scenarios in my mind.

'If you need to call a client, this screen has all client details. This screen here is your diary to book my clients. I have access to it on my laptop,' he explains.

'Brooke is my assistant downstairs. Call her. Her number is on the desk if you need anything,' he says.

'Okay.'

'I'll get her to bring you a skirt-suit, blouse, pantyhose, and court shoes. There is a staff bathroom down the hall to the right. Have a shower, get changed, and put some makeup on,' he says, smiling before leaving.

'Okay,' I say, smiling at his hospitality. Ten minutes later, Brooke comes upstairs with a cream blouse, navy skirt-suit, black pantyhose, and black court shoes in my size.

'Hello, I believe these are for you,' she says, smiling. 'I'm Brooke.'

'Brooke, nice to meet you. I'm Astrid. Thank you,' I say, taking the outfit from her. Brooke is slim, petite, and has blonde hair and blue eyes. She wears a navy skirt suit too.

'I have to go now, but if you need anything, call me,' she says, smiling and going downstairs. I go into the bathroom, shower, and admire the gorgeous corporate attire, hanging it on a hook. The hot water stings parts of my skin but feels glorious. It is precisely what I need after an exhausting morning. I push my feet into the black pantyhose and pull them up over my hips, letting the black elasticised waistband rest on my stomach. They're not too tight, and they fit perfectly. I step into the navy skirt and zip it. It fits me perfectly, like a glove. The cream blouse is silk. I tuck it into the top of the waist-high skirt and revel in how it feels against my skin.

   I push my arms into the structured sleeves of the gorgeous navy blazer and step into the court shoes, which are my size. There is a brush and a bag of cosmetics under the bathroom sink. Once I brush my hair, I scoop it up into a scrunched bun before applying some foundation, eyeliner, mascara, and red lipstick and look at myself in the mirror. I feel and look good. My old clothes, socks, and shoes are on the Bathroom Vanity. With one final coat of red lipstick on my lips, I stuff the gold-encased lipstick into my blazer pocket and push the bathroom door open.

   I'm just about to sit at the desk when a man enters. I know him straight away to be James, John's twin brother. He looks me up and down like I'm a snack and whistles.

   'You accepted Dad's job offer, I see,' he says with a grin.

   'I did. It's a pleasure to meet you, James,' I politely say.

'The pleasure is all mine,' he says, taking my hand and kissing it. He winks at me and walks to the office to the right of Zeniths before stopping and turning to look at me.

'In case you are unsure, this is my office. The one on the other side of Dad's is John's. So, we work together sometimes in Dad's office,' he says, smiling.

Nodding, I smile. The phone rings, and I answer it in my best professional voice.

'Zenith Creations. Astrid is speaking. How may I help you?' I say.

'It's Dom Hayes. I need to see Zenith as soon as possible.'

'Okay, sir. Please hold on a moment,' I open the diary screen and find a free spot tomorrow.

'Mr. Hayes,' I offer, 'I can book you in for 2 pm tomorrow?'

'Okay, I'll see him tomorrow,' Mr Hayes says, ending the call before I can say goodbye. I spend the day answering calls from clients, booking appointments, and passing on messages. I see John and James leaning over my desk halfway through the day, looking at me with coy expressions.

'Is there something I can help you with?' I ask them.

'Astrid, there is something you can do. If you could follow me into my office,' John says. James elbows him playfully.

'Don't mind him. He is just stirring,' James says.

'We would love a coffee,' James says, winking and smiling.

'How would you like your coffee?' I ask, ignoring John's smirks.

'Latte, no sugar. John will have the same.'

'Okay.' I walk into the kitchen and look at the enormous copper industrial coffee machine sitting on the granite benchtop. *How am I meant to use this thing?* I recall what I learned in my six-hour barista class a few years ago. I surprised myself and made the coffees expertly. I place the mugs and teaspoon on a tray and carry it to the men. I put the lattes down in front of them. They're impressed.

'Won't your father be angry you are out here staring at me instead of working?' I ask. James grins.

'You're right, Astrid,' he says, gives me a wink, and returns to his office with his latte.

'John, get back to work,' he laughs. John returns to his office with his latte.

'You know how to handle those two, don't you?' Brooke giggles. 'You must tell me about yourself. How old are you? Where are you from?' She asks.

'I'll be eighteen in five days. I used to live with my dad, a forty-five-minute walk from here,' I reply.

'How exciting! You'll meet your wolf this week!' She says excitedly. I give a fake smile.

'Yeah, so excited...' I say with a tinge of sarcasm and sadness—the phone rings.

'I better get back to my desk downstairs,' Brooke says, running downstairs in her court shoes. I answer the phone.

'Zenith Creations. Astrid is speaking. How may I help you?' I ask.

'It's me. Zenith. Make us both a latte and bring them to my office,' he says, ending the call. I push open his door with the lattes in my hands and put them on his desk.

'You've done well today, Astrid,' he says.

'Thank you,' I reply, sipping my latte.

'We need to discuss your living arrangements. You can stay in the packhouse with the boys and me if you're comfortable doing so,' Zenith offers.

I pause in thought at his offer. *I don't have anywhere to stay, and I don't want to live with his sons. So, what choice do I have?*

'Okay, just for now, though,' I smile, accepting his offer.

'Good. It's settled then,' Zenith smiles, sipping his latte.

At 5 pm, I follow Zenith to the elevator. John and James follow behind.

'You can hop in with me,' James offers, smiling.

'Thank you. I'll go with your Dad,' I say, smiling.

I get into Zenith's car. A vital phone call takes his attention for the duration of our ride home. Finally, we arrive, and I see a sign that reads *Shady Crest*. I gulp. Wait, *this is the Pack Vanessa and Alice lived! The Pack abused Vanessa and used her as the pack slave.*

'Is something wrong?' John asks, staring at me.

'No, I'm just admiring the house. It's so lovely,' I say, trying to contain my nerves. His house is large and impressive. It's not as big as Ryker's, but still gorgeous. The car stops. Zenith opens his door and helps me out. My court shoes crunch on pristine white gravel.

'Are you okay, Astrid? You're shaking,' he says.

'I'm fine. I'm cold,' I lie, rubbing my arms.

'Let's go inside.'

We walk up the twenty stone steps to a glossy green front door and walk inside into a foyer. Zenith puts his black leather case on a nearby table with his coat.

'This way, to the dining room', he says, smiling. I follow him into the dining room. People sit at a long mahogany table and are served plates of food by employees.

Everyone goes quiet and stands with Zenith's arrival.

'I'd like to introduce you all to Astrid formally,' he says, placing a hand on my back. There are a few gasps and whispers among them.

'Silence,' Zenith says calmly.

'Astrid is staying with us. Hopefully, she will join our Pack too. I know I can count on you to make her feel welcome and at home,' he says, with utmost authority in his voice.

Zenith walks to his chair at the head of the table.

'Astrid, you may dine next to me tonight.' he says. I nod and sit in the chair next to him. All eyes are on me. I look around the table and give a nervous but friendly smile.

They all smile and nod. I realise they're excited I'm here. I eat, and the Pack members introduce themselves to me. James sits next to me, and John sits opposite me. The pretty girl next to John shakes my hand.

'I'm Amelia, John's mate,' she says, smiling. I look at John, tilting my head in surprise.

'John, you never mentioned you had a mate,' I say.

'Oh, didn't I?' He says. James smirks.

'I suppose you have a mate too, then?' I ask James. He smiles while eating.

'No, I haven't. Dad is telling me to choose one, though,' he says, winking and brushing my leg with his under the table. I blush and look away.

'Amelia, I'd love you to give me a tour of the house,' I say, smiling at her.

'I would love to, Astrid,' she replies with a smile. We finish our meals, and she skips around the table and links her arm with mine. 'Let's tour,' she says excitedly.

Strange that Vanessa said she was once a slave here and beaten. Everyone seems pretty civilised here. Everyone has been amicable. I might even get used to the boys flirting. I'm sure I can find out more information through Amelia.

'This is the dining room,' she giggles. She shows me through the kitchen, hallways, and upstairs bedrooms.

'This is my room, mine and John's. This room over here is vacant. You can take this room if you like, then we will be near each other,' she says excitedly.

'Sure. I'll take it,' I say, smiling. The room is pleasant and straightforward. Unfortunately, it doesn't have a bathroom.

'Where would I find the bathroom?' I ask.

'Only the highest ranks here get a bathroom. There are a couple of communal bathrooms, two doors up and the other down the hall. James' bedroom is next to yours if you need anything,' she smiles.

'Oh, thanks. That's great,' I say, hiding my unease.

'You brought nothing with you. I'll give you a nightie to wear,' she says, crossing the hallway to her room.

'Thanks.' I smile and accept the nightie and towels she gives me.

'Here you go,' she says. 'Have a good sleep. I'll see you tomorrow,' she says, skipping to her room. Once in the bathroom, I lock the door behind me and shower. I step out into the corridor and explore. It's just bedrooms and bathrooms, so I return to my room and sit by the window.

'Moon Goddess, I know I've only just learnt you exist and that I know little about you. Please watch over Ryker. I miss him so much and wish things were different and will treasure the short time we had together, how he would gaze into my eyes, and how he would hold me tenderly. I am so grateful you matched us as mates, but I'm sorry it cannot be.'

Pushing myself up from the floor, I fold a blanket back and climb into bed for much-needed rest.

CHAPTER 12

I can barely sleep. Ryker is on my mind all night. I'm apprehensive and nervous about my first shift in four days. After a yawn and a stretch, I get dressed, make the bed, and go downstairs to the dining room for breakfast. A few members are already at the table eating. Amelia is one of them.

'Good morning, Astrid,' she says.

'Good morning, everyone,' I say, sitting beside Amelia. The other ladies smile.

'You'll have to tell me all about Shady Crest,' I tell Amelia.

'Alpha Zenith is obviously our Alpha,' she giggles.

'Yep. I think I got that.' I chuckle.

'We train here daily, including she-wolves. Alpha Zenith likes to keep our reputation intact. We're the strongest pack, and he wants us prepared if another pack becomes a threat so that we can take them out. His eldest son James hasn't found his mate yet. Alpha Zenith has one in mind. He won't say who just yet, but says he will only settle for the strongest she-wolf, as James will eventually take over as Alpha,' she explains.

'What if James finds his true mate in the meantime?' I ask.

'Alpha Zenith is part of the council called the elders. They have the power to vote and choose an Alpha's mate for them if they feel their current mate is inadequate. If they don't suit as Luna or don't benefit the pack,' she explains.

Alpha Zenith is part of the Elders' council! Ryker said they had wanted Vanessa as Ryker's mate. Why would Alpha Zenith make Vanessa Luna of Shadow Crest when she was the pack slave here at Shady Crest? It makes little sense.

'That's terrible, to remove someone's true mate. A mate that the Moon Goddess chose for you. Love is all that should matter. Being with your true mate, your one true love,' I say, feeling my eyes well up, thinking of Ryker.

'Amelia? Where is Alpha Zenith's mate? Where is the Luna of Shady Crest?' I ask. Amelia bites her lip and looks at the other two ladies sitting at the table eating breakfast.

'Um, you see—' They quickly stand and bow their heads. Alpha Zenith walks into the room.

'Astrid. Good to see you're ready for work,' he smiles.

'Good morning,' I reply nervously. Other pack members approach the table for breakfast once we finish eating, and I follow Zenith to his car.

I sat in the back of the Mercedes with Zenith this morning. There is no sign of John or James.

'Is John not joining us?' I ask.

'No, he will go in his car today.'

'Oh, okay,' I say.

'I want to discuss some things privately with you,' he says. I'm nervous and don't know what to expect.

'It's your eighteenth in four days,' he says.

'Yes, that's correct,' I say. Zenith rubs his missing half ear in thought. I want to ask him about it but don't want to be rude.

'You would be a great asset to my pack, Astrid. When you turn eighteen, you'll be able to sense your mate,' he states.

'Yes, I know,' I say, unsure of where he is going with this.

'You know my son James hasn't found his mate yet and is of age.'

'What does it have to do with me?' I ask.

'What would you say if I wanted you to be John's mate?' He asks.

'I-I'm flattered, but I would prefer to find my true mate.'

'What if you don't find him?' He asks.

'What if I do?' I retort. He lets out a chuckle.

'Oh, Astrid, you are a stubborn one! Perhaps think about the idea for a few days,' he smiles.

'Why would you want someone weak like me to be your son's mate? Wouldn't you want a strong she-wolf to bear his pups?' I ask.

'You'll find out why I'm asking when you shift into your wolf on your birthday,' he says, still smiling. *What is he talking about? And mate with James! I don't want to be with anyone other than Ryker, even if Ryker moves on with Vanessa. Just the thought of being with someone else makes me feel nauseous.*

We arrive at the underground car park and ascend in the elevator in silence. I take my seat at my desk and start answering phone calls. John and James go into their dad's office. James winks at me as he walks past.

'Zenith Creations. Astrid is speaking. How may I help you?' I say.

'Tell the boss I got his special delivery here he ordered,' the caller says.

'Okay, and who is speaking?' I ask.

'Beta Glen,' he replies. I place Beta Glen on hold and call Zenith.

'Beta Glen says he has your special delivery here,' I inform him.

'Tell him to bring him up right away.'

'Okay.' I press the button for Glen.

'Zenith says bring him up right away.' I hang up the phone. *That is weird referring to the order as him.*

The elevator dings, and my jaw drops. Two men in suits drag a third into the room. The man's hands are bound behind his back with rope, and he has a calico bag over his head. New and old blood stain the man's shirt. I contain a gasp. They drag the man past me nonchalantly and into Zenith's office. I hear the odd thump and agonized moans. It's quite confronting.

The phone rings, and I answer it. It's Zenith.

'Make lattes please,' he says before hanging up. I gulp at the thought of going into the room. I don't want to see what's going on in there.

I place five lattes on a tray and carry them to his office, using my hip to push the door open. I set the five lattes on the desk. All five men stare at me. Zenith wipes his hands clean on a wet rag. The man is unconscious on the ground.

I stare wide in horror and bite my tongue. I can only see his back, but it's enough to know they've beaten him.

'Oh, don't worry about him, Astrid. He will be fine,' Zenith smiles.

'Beta Glen and Gamma Dan, Astrid,' he says, introducing the men to me. My voice shakes as I stare at the man on the floor.

'It's nice to meet you both,' I say nervously, avoiding eye contact.

'This isn't *the Astrid*, is it Zenith? The Astrid from Moon—' Glen coughs after Zenith strikes him across the head.

'Not another word, Glen,' Zenith snaps. His tone is deep and creepy. I jump back in fright. Zenith watches me back away slowly.

'Please don't mind Glen here. He forgets his manners sometimes, and I need to remind him,' he says, trying to calm me.

'Take him back to the basement!' He snaps. Glen and Dan put the calico bag back over the man's head and drag him out of the office toward the elevator. I watch in horror and jump when a hand gently squeezes my shoulder. It's James.

'Sorry, you had to see that, Astrid. I told Dad it wasn't a good idea, but he says it will toughen you up when you're my mate,' James says. I step back and glare at Zenith.

'I never agreed to that,' I say.

'I told you it would toughen her up,' Zenith says, grinning. James is crestfallen.

Angry, I run out of the office and into the bathroom, locking myself in a cubicle. I'm hyperventilating. The bathroom door creaks open. I place my hands over my mouth so whoever is here cannot hear me.

'Astrid, let's go home,' James says. I don't want to go anywhere with James. I only want Ryker.

Closing my eyes, I imagine myself in Ryker's arms with my head against his chest, listening to his heartbeat. James taps the cubicle door, disrupting my daydream. I unlock the door, swing it open, and storm out toward the elevator.

At the last second, Zenith hops into the elevator with us. The elevator dings, and we descend. No one says anything. Outside in the car park, John waits in his car. Zenith opens his car door, gesturing for me to hop in. I stare at the open door, hesitating, and look at James.

'You can always come with me,' he says. But, of course, I don't want to be near any of them. Zenith is impatient now. He grabs my arm and pulls me into the back seat.

'Get in! I'm not waiting around,' he snaps.

Falling onto the seat, I let out a cry. I sit as far away from Zenith as possible and look out the window, avoiding conversation. His phone rings on the way.

'What kind of problem? ... I see ... do you think his mate will return? ... Good ... Vanessa, now listen to me... yes, you will! I'm your father! I don't care what you have to do. Bear his pups! Drug him if you must. Alice will put it in his food. I've waited long enough!' I'm shocked by what

I'm hearing. *So, Vanessa is his daughter, and Alice is the Luna of Shady Crest? Zenith never enslaved them!*

'I don't care if he doesn't want you. This isn't about love. It's about power. If we want to expand and become the greatest pack, you need to bear his pups, kill him and combine packs.' Zenith sees my horrified expression. Colour drains from my face.

He squints and studies me for a moment.

'Vanessa, what's his mate's name?' He asks.

My stomach churns. I'm going to be sick. No one can help me. Jim's diner is up the road. I pull the handle on the car door, but it won't open because it's locked. Vanessa has told him my name. Zenith laughs at my struggles. *I'm just a pawn in his game.* I punch the windows, to no avail.

'Vanessa, she won't be a problem and won't be returning to Shadow Crest. I have her with me right now,' he says, laughing.

'Oh, Astrid, the windows are bulletproof. Give it up already, honey,' he says, placing his hand on my leg.

'Don't touch me!' I yell.

'Vanessa, I need to go. Your brothers betrothed needs to be put in her place. Yes, that's right. Why? Because I said so! You'll find out in a few days,' he says, ending the call.

Slumped in the seat, defeated, Zenith leaps forward, grabs me aggressively by the hair, and yanks me toward him.

'You never told me Alpha Ryker was your mate! You'll let James mark you after your first shift. Vanessa is to be Alpha Ryker's mate,' he shouts.

He releases me and shoves me back into the seat. Tears run down my face. The car stops outside the packhouse. Zenith gets out of the car and waits for me to get out. He even holds out his hand to me, which I do not want to take.

'Don't make this difficult, Astrid! He yelled, 'I will drag you out if I have to!' I ignore him. I kick and scream when he leans in and tries to grab me.

'Don't touch me! Get away from me!' James and John are standing behind him.

'Dad! What is going on?' James asks.

'This little whore of yours is being difficult.' he says, successfully grabbing my leg and yanking me out of the car by my ankle.

I hit the ground with force, cried out, and rolled a few metres across the gravel. My arms and legs have scrapes, and my tights are laddered and torn. Zenith, John, and James stare at me with black eyes.

CHAPTER 13

I discard my heels and run in my tights as fast as possible.

'Get her boys!' Zenith yells. John and James shift and chase me in their wolf forms. I run through the trees and slip, rolling down a rocky hill.

My hair is messy, with leaves and twigs sticking out at many angles. I continue to run.

'Ryker!' I scream at the top of my lungs. Someone hazardously throws me down. I kick and punch them as hard as I can. A hand covers my mouth. The weight of a body holds me down. He is completely naked now, in his human form.

'Shh... shh,' James whispers, stroking my face. I can't free myself. My movements are futile.

'Stop trying to fight me,' he whispers. Tears roll down my cheeks.

'Consummating the pairing already?' John laughs.

'Fuck off, John,' he says to his brother.

'Why did you scream out for Ryker?' James asks. He slowly removes his hand, and I spit in his face. John laughs.

'You better put her in her place before Dad does, James! You know he won't tolerate her treating you like that,' John warns. James looks at me and wipes the spit from his face with his free hand.

'Look, if you're going to be soft about it, I'll put her in her place for you,' James says.

'Tell me, Astrid. Why did you call out for Ryker?' He asks. I want to spit in his face again, but he covers my mouth with his hand before I can.

'Astrid, I don't want to hurt you, but you will leave me no choice if you don't answer me,' he snaps.

He removes his hand from my mouth. I look away. He holds my jaw in one hand, forcing me to look at him.

'Answer me, Astrid. This is your last warning,' he says. I look James dead in the eyes.

'Alpha Ryker is my mate! And I'm the Luna of Shadow Crest! I suggest you take your hands off me before Ryker finds out where I am and rips you apart, limb by limb!' I threaten. James growls in anger.

'You're my mate! Not his!' He says. 'Why didn't the Moon Goddess bless me with a mate like you? Why did she bless *Alpha Ryker* with you?' He asks, frustrated.

'Maybe because she doesn't like you!' I say, kneeing him in the crotch. He falls back in pain. I quickly wiggle myself from under him and start running again.

'Save the feistiness for the bedroom!' James yells while John chases me in his wolf form. My foot catches on something, and I fall face-first into the ground. I try to get up, but John presses his foot into my back, keeping me down. He sits on me and moves my hair away from my neck to inhale my scent. He emits a lustful growl.

'Why should James have all the fun?' He says, rolling me onto my back and gazing into my eyes.

'Why are you doing this? You have your mate. You have Amelia!' I yell.

'You're so beautiful. I might need to help myself to a bite,' John says. His wolf's fangs protrude, and his face lingers near my throat.

I scream as he is about to sink his teeth into my neck. His eyes were full of hunger. Then a flash appears out of nowhere. James pulls John off me.

'Are you fucking crazy?' He yells at John.

'Not only did you almost mark *my* mate, but you would also have killed Amelia for marking another she-wolf!' James yells.

'I'm sorry. I couldn't help it. Don't tell Amelia,' John begs.

'I will not tell her anything. It's Astrid you need to worry about with Amelia.'

I let them discuss their issues and run again. They shift, catch me again, and James knocks me down. He holds my arms behind my back in human form.

'Enough, Astrid!' He snaps, lifting me with my arms still restrained so I can't hit him. He holds me closer to his naked chest and carries me back to the packhouse.

'About bloody time! Bring her downstairs!' Zenith growls, walking down the staircase.

'To the cells?' James questions.

'Do you expect her to stay in her room obediently?' He asks.

'No, but—' he says.

'She'll keep in the cell until you have marked her. Then, she won't be able to escape.' John and James follow Zenith downstairs to the basement. It's dark and eerie, and I can hear water trickling in the walls and the squeaking sounds of mice. Our exhalations are misty in the coldness. I'm shivering. James pulls me closer to keep me warm.

Zenith unlocks a cell door. James walks in and places me on a stone bench. Chains with silver cuffs adorn the walls, and I'm thankful James doesn't cuff me.

He kisses me on the forehead instead, making me shudder.

'It'll be okay, Astrid. We have some things to sort out. The sooner you let me mark you, the sooner we can get you out of this cell,' he says, cradling my face in his hands. I jerk my head out of his grasp.

James leaves and stands beside John. Zenith comes into the cell and strikes me aggressively across the face.

'Try to run away again, and that split lip of yours will be the least of your worries!' He snaps. He slams the loud, creaking metal door closed, and the sound reverberates around the basement. He locks the door with a key.

I hug my knees on the bench as they walk away. It's dirty and cold where I sit. The stone wall behind me is full of cobwebs. The few other cells I can see are the same. It's pitch black, and not even moonlight comes in. My arms and legs sting from all the abrasions, but I can't see them.

'Ryker, I'm scared. I'm so scared. Please save me! I want to be back in your arms!' I cry out, but no one can hear.

At midnight, I'm still awake and freezing to death. I hear light footsteps coming downstairs. I squint toward the stairs to see who it is.

'Astrid, it's me, Amelia,' she whispers. Jumping up, I run to the cell door.

'Amelia! Please, Amelia! Please help me. Please unlock the door,' I beg.

'Shh! I'm not supposed to be down here. I'll get into trouble if anyone finds out,' she whispers. She passes me my hoodie from my room.

'I thought you'd need this. I know how cold it gets down here,' Amelia says.

'Have they put you down here before?' I ask. Amelia nods.

'It was a long time ago. Alpha Zenith bought me from my old pack. Then, he chose me as John's mate. So, I had to stay down here until John marked me,' she says sadly.

'John isn't your fated mate?' I ask in disbelief.

'No. And I haven't been able to leave the packhouse since. If I found my true mate, he wouldn't want me now. I'm marked and mated by another,' she sobs.

'Oh Amelia, I'm so sorry,' I empathically say.

'I overheard James and Alpha Zenith arguing about you upstairs. Instead of down here, James is begging him to let him chain you up in his room. That's how I knew you were down here,' she whispers. We hold hands through the bars.

'I don't want you to have the same fate as me, Astrid. So, I will do everything to help you out of here,' she says, as her eyes go glassy with tears.

'I have to go now. I'll come back when everyone is asleep tomorrow night. Don't let him mark you, no matter what,' she says as she walks away.

I examine the cell and rattle every bar, hoping to find a flaw so I can break free and escape. But, to my dismay, none of the metal bars moves or budge.

The ground is mainly dirt. I scoop dirt away from the back of the cell. After an hour of digging with my hands, I hit a large stone.

I'm left defeated with no way out. I curl up on the cold stone bench and hug myself. Even with my hoodie, it's still freezing. My teeth chatter, and I eventually fall asleep.

Jazz Ford

CHAPTER 14

Alpha Ryker

I'm excited about spending the day with Astrid. Every day, she trusts me more and more. She is thankfully adjusting to werewolf life. After my shower, I knock on her door. There's no answer. I knock again.

'Astrid, are you awake?' I open the door. Her bed is neat and creaseless. She hasn't slept in it. *Strange.* I knock on the ensuite door. She isn't there either. One of her drawers is open. Inside, Astrid's clothes are strewn about the room. She must have been in a hurry. My stomach sinks. Her bag is gone. I sprint downstairs to the dining room. Seth and Mia are at the table with Kane, Hayley, and Vanessa. They all stand as I enter.

'Has anyone seen Astrid?' I ask. They shrug and say they haven't.

'Is she still asleep?' Mia asks.

'No, she isn't there, and her bag is gone too,' I say in a panic.

'Ryker, I'm sure she's around somewhere. I'll mind-link the pack to keep an eye out for her,' Seth suggests. I call out for Astrid, running through the house, searching every room and end up back in the dining room.

'She isn't in the house!' I panic.

'Alpha Ryker, your breakfast is ready,' Alice says.

'You haven't seen Astrid, have you, Alice?' I ask.

'No, Alpha, I've been in the kitchen since 6 am. She smiles and says she hasn't seen her. I run out the front door and pick up her scent. I rip my clothes off, shift into my wolf, let out a loud, sad howl and race toward Astrid's scent. An hour later, I'm deep in the woods when her scent vanishes. I run in different directions, becoming more and more distressed. *Astrid, I don't understand why you'd leave me. Where would you go?* I think about where she might have gone. The diner is the only place Astrid would go. There's no way she would have gone back to her Dad. I run to the diner and shift back into my human form, not caring that I'm completely naked.

'Jim!' I shout. 'Jim!' All the customers freeze in shock at my nudity. An overweight man catches his wife grinning. He covers her eyes with his hands and gives me an unimpressed look.

'Ryker! Damn it. Get some clothes on! We're full of customers!' Jim yells.

'Astrid! Have you seen her?' I ask in a rush.

'No, I haven't seen her since she left with you,' he says.

'Shit! She's missing. Her bag is gone. I don't know why she would run away,' I panic.

'I'll call you if I see her. But, in the meantime, you need to leave. My female customers are gawking, and their husbands want to give you a black eye!' Jim says.

Frustrated, I leave the diner and shift back into my wolf, searching the woods, hoping to pick up her scent and find nothing, not a trace of her anywhere. I mind-link Seth and Kane and tell them to organise search parties. I don't return home for 24 hours until I have no choice but to rest. Afterwards, I continue searching for her.

In bed, a hand rests on my chest.

'Astrid!' I sit up and see Vanessa asleep in my bed next to me. I let out a loud growl, waking her up.

'Ryker, don't growl at me! It would help if you got over her. Astrid left because she doesn't love you. Astrid doesn't want you or the responsibility of being Luna,' Vanessa says.

'Get out of my bed and out of my room now, Vanessa!' I yell.

'Fine! But eventually, you will have to accept me as your chosen mate, whether or not you like it! You know the elders don't want a weak runaway as Luna!' She says, getting out of my bed.

Jumping out of bed, I pin Vanessa to the wall with my hand around her neck.

'Don't you ever call my mate weak again! Do you hear me?' I yell.

'Ryker, you're hurting me,' she says. I let go, letting her drop to the floor. She holds her neck and looks up at me, her eyes well.

'Get out now and never return to the Packhouse!' I yell. She stands and runs out of the room.

Making my way downstairs, I find Seth.

'Alpha Ryker, we had five search parties look for her while you slept. We found no trace of her. We will keep searching until we find her, Alpha.' Nodding, I sit at the dining table.

'Seth, tell Alice to be quick with the food. I need to continue looking for Astrid,' I order. Seth nods and retreats to the kitchen. Moments later, Alice brings me a plate of food and puts it on the table in front of me.

'Alpha Ryker! I'm very displeased with your behaviour toward my daughter. She has done nothing wrong. Why can't you accept her as your chosen mate? At least she won't run away!' Alice snaps.

Glaring at Alice, I let out a growl of warning.

'Alice, I suggest you get back in the kitchen because my wolf is not in the mood today to tolerate you or your daughter! And I suggest you accept that Vanessa will never be my mate!' I snap back. Alice glares at me and storms back to the kitchen. I finish my meal and walk out the door, adamant I'll find Astrid.

'Alpha Ryker!' I see one of my best warriors, Leon, racing toward me.

'Leon,' I greet him.

'Alpha Ryker, we have some good news and some bad news. First, we picked up Astrid's scent in the city. It's faint, but it's her. The bad news is we haven't found her yet, but with this lead, we'll hopefully have your mate home soon,' he says. *So what would Astrid be doing in the city? She doesn't know anyone there.*

'Excellent, Leon. I'll join you in the city. Show me where you picked up her scent,' I command.

'I'll get Seth to drive us. It would be quicker in wolf form, but we can't look for her naked,' Leon points out. Nodding, I mind-link Seth to get the car. On the way there,

I'm hopeful we'll find her. *I should have her back in my arms today. I want to inhale her scent, feel the sparks between us, and taste her lips.*

We split up when we arrive in the city. It's her scent, but it's so faint that we can't follow it. So, I decided we'll spend the day in the city looking for her.

Mind-linking Leon and Seth, I tell them: *Maybe she is working in a shop? It might be worth looking in the stores for her.* I enter hundreds of stores. There is no sign of her, and I can't trace her scent anywhere else.

Nightfall nears when Seth mind-links me and says he'll stay the night in the city to keep searching. Leon drives me back to the house for food and rest, promising to return in the morning when we will take over from Seth.

It's an arduous drive home. I was so sure we would find Astrid today. Finally, arriving, Alice opens the front door.

'Alpha Ryker, I want to apologise for this morning. Unfortunately, I was out of line. I hope you'll forgive me,' she says. I can't be bothered arguing with her. Forgiveness is easier.

'I forgive you, Alice, if you accept Astrid as your Luna,' Alice pauses in thought and nods.

'Of course, Alpha,' she says with a hesitant smile.

'I made a special dinner for you tonight, Alpha,' she says.

She was gesturing to the food on the table. I sat at the table and ate alone. Everyone else ate and left before I got home. After eating, I feel unnaturally tired.

CHAPTER 15

'Alpha, you look tired.

May I suggest you rest for the night?' Alice says. I nod, making my way to my room—everything in my room sways. I grab onto the armchair and sit down. Kicking my shoes off, I wait for the swaying to stop. My door creaks open.

'Is someone there?' I ask, squinting at the figure I can barely make out.

'It's me!' She says.

'Astrid? Is that you?' I ask and try to stand, but my balance is off. I feel a hand gently press against my chest.

'Sit down, Ryker. I'm here now. I'll take care of you,' she whispers. She straddles herself on my lap.

'Astrid, you came back.'

'Of course, I did,' she whispers as she slowly unbuttons my shirt.

'Why did you leave? Where did you go?' I ask.

'All that matters is that I'm here with you.'

One hand caresses my bare chest while her other unfastens my belt. Her lips brush across mine.

'Ryker,' she whispers lustfully, placing my hands on either side of her thighs.

'Astrid,' I whisper.

'I want you to mark me, Ryker,' she whispers.

Everything spins and sways, and I'm in an absolute stupor. All I can think of is making love to her.

'I'm going to mark you first,' she whispers seductively in my ear. Her teeth protrude and scrape the skin on my neck. I feel the pressure as she is about to puncture my neck. *But, wait. Astrid can't shift yet. She can't mark me yet. Where's our usual heat? Sparks?* I quickly push the person off of me.

'Alpha! What's wrong?' She asks.

'Vanessa?' I ask, squinting to adjust my sight.

'No, it's Astrid,' she says.

I try to stand.

'Vanessa! Astrid hasn't had her first shift yet. She can't mark me even if she wanted to!' I yell in anger and fall to the ground.

'What have you done to me?' I yell.

'Ryker, please! Astrid is not coming back. I'm doing you and the pack a favour!' She yells. I try to mind-link Leon and Kane, but I can't connect.

'Did you poison me?' I ask.

'Not exactly,' she says. I try to crawl towards my door. But unfortunately, I'm about to lose consciousness and fall into darkness before getting to it.

'He is too heavy, mum. We can't even roll him,' Vanessa says. I squint, letting my eyes adjust. I haven't moved from my spot on the floor.

My head is pounding, and nausea creeps over me. I mind-link Leon and Kane for help. I'm still groggy but can see clearer.

'Quick, do it now, Vanessa!' Alice yells, shoving Vanessa toward me.

Vanessa straddles me and bares her fangs over my neck. I want to push her off, but Alice hits me across the head with a heavy object. Her fangs caress my nape when Leon and Kane barge in and pull her off me.

'Alpha! Are you okay?' Kane asks.

'They drugged me! Vanessa almost marked me,' I yell, angered.

'You have waited too long for your Luna. Vanessa would be a more fitting Luna than that wretched little bitch Astrid!' Alice yells.

Standing, I lean against the wall for support.

'Bring Alice to me now!' I snap. Leon has Alice's arms behind her back and pushes her toward me. I grip her neck tightly with my hand.

'What did you do to Astrid? Where is she?' I yell. Alice struggles to breathe but forces a smile at my words. I squeeze her neck tighter.

'I will kill you right now if you do not tell me!' I warn.

She struggles for breath and gives a slight nod. I release my grip—enough for her to speak.

'The morning she disappeared, she came into the kitchen for something to eat. No one else was up yet. I told Astrid to save herself the heartbreak of the elders choosing Vanessa over her and to leave and that if she refused to leave, I would kill her anyway before her first shift.'

My wolf growls ferociously in her face. I'm struggling to control my wolf. As much as I want to see Alice dead, killing Alice won't bring Astrid back. I throw her across the room.

'Kane! Leon! Take them both to the cells, where they will stay!' I yell. I sit back in the armchair.

Leon and Kane return a short while later with a jug of water and a glass. They place them on the table next to me.

'Alice must have drugged my food. I felt dizzy after eating it. I couldn't even stand up straight. Vanessa pretended to be Astrid, and she seduced me. She wanted to mark me,' I explain. Leon and Kane look at each other with worry.

'Alpha, rest in bed today until it wears off,' Kane says.

'No, we need to find Astrid! Have any of you heard from Seth?' I ask.

'No. We'll go into the city. We'll take over from him. You won't be much help, Alpha, in your condition,' Leon says.

Sculling two large glasses of water, I stand.

'I'm fine,' I say, only to fall back into the armchair.

'Come on, Alpha,' Leon says, grabbing one arm and Kane the other, lifting me over to my bed.

'Rest Alpha. We'll mind-link you the moment we hear anything or find her. I'll have Hayley and Mia check on you throughout the day. Mind-link them if you need anything,' Kane says. They leave, and not long after that, I'm asleep.

I wake that afternoon and mind-link them. *'Any progress?'* I ask. *'I don't know how to tell you this, Alpha, but we haven't been able to mind-link Seth or find him. He has gone awol,'* Kane links.

Attempting to mind-link Seth myself, nothing happens. *Something must have happened to him. He wouldn't just disappear. He would have mind-linked us.* I link Kane and Leon. *Keep searching for them both. Keep trying to mind-link Seth. I will be in the city soon. And yes, I'm feeling much better, so I will be of use.*

We spent all night searching for Astrid and Seth. *I don't understand. Astrid has vanished without a trace, and now Seth? What if someone is involved in their disappearance? Who? There are only two nights until Astrid shifts. I need to find her now.*

Returning home, I want to feel as close to Astrid as possible. So, I go into her room and look around. Her scent is overpowering on the couch.

Wanting to be close to Astrid, I lie on the couch, and a few thoughts cross my mind. *Astrid has been sleeping here instead of in her bed. It smells like vanilla and cookies. It explains why her bed looks as fresh as the day she arrived. So why wouldn't she sleep in the bed?*

Drifting off to sleep on the couch, I dream of Astrid. I kiss her lips and look into her beautiful green eyes.

'Astrid, my mate. I have been blessed the Moon Goddess chose us to be together,' I say.

'Ryker, I want to be by your side forever,' she whispers, looking into my eyes. Then, before we can kiss, she disappears from my arms. 'Astrid! Wait! Come back! Astrid!' I sit upright on the couch and look around the quiet room.

It was just a dream. I stare at the floor, finding a business card. *Zenith Creations. We were near that building yesterday! Why would Astrid be at Zenith Creations? How does she even know Alpha Zenith? That pack has always been bad news!* I mind-link Kane and Leon. *'Get the car ready. I think I know where Astrid is!'* I put the card in my pocket. Walking outside, I get in the car.

'Where are we going?' Kane asks.

'Zenith Creations,' I say. Kane and Leon give each other a look.

'What has Alpha Zenith got to do with Astrid?' Kane asks.

'We're about to find out,' I reply.

CHAPTER 16

Astrid

'Astrid, you need to eat,' James says. Ignoring him, I keep my eyes on the stone floor. This will be my second night down in the cell. I've refused all food and never acknowledged James's presence when he comes down to the cell.

He punches the cell door angrily. I flinch in fright. I'm worried.

'Damn it, Astrid! Why can't you be a good little mate and do what you're told?' He yells.

Hearing keys, James unlocks the cell. It creaks open. James picks me up and sits on the bench, holding me tightly in his lap. I try to fight him off. I scratch his cheek. He slaps me hard across the face and wraps his arms tightly around me so I can't move. His nose nuzzles my hair and sniffs the back of my neck.

'Astrid, I could make you so happy if you let me,' he says.

'You will never think of Alpha Ryker again if you give me a chance,' he whispers. I wriggle and squirm. 'After your first shift, I will mark you straight away,' he says. I stiffen at his words.

'No, I won't let you. You can't mark me. I belong with Ryker.'

'You may not like the thought of it now, but you will learn to love me,' he says.

'I will never love you, James! So, you better start getting that into your thick head!' I yell.

'Finally! You speak,' he says with a chuckle. 'Two more nights and your wolf will be here. Perhaps I'll watch your first shift. Hmm?' he says.

'I'd rather you go jump off a cliff!' I say.

'Now, now,' he says, moving my hair away from my shoulder. He plants kisses along my shoulder.

'Stop!' I yell and squirm. James lets out a sigh and places me on the stone bench.

'I will be back tomorrow to spend more bonding time with you,' he smiles.

I cross my arms in disapproval as he leaves the cell and locks the door.

'Goodnight, Astrid.' he says, walking away. I lie down facing the cell door, cradling myself. I have to get out of here.

A few hours later, Amelia tiptoes softly downstairs. She lets out a sigh of relief when she sees James hasn't marked me yet.

'Alpha Zenith is going back into the city tomorrow for business. James and John will also be going. I'll look for the cell keys. I'll get you out of here,' she says with a smile.

Nodding, I'm hoping her plan works. Through the gaps of the bars, I take her hand.

'Come with me!' I offer. Amelia looks taken back.

'I can't leave. John and Zenith will hunt me down,' she says sadly, looking away.

'Let them! Alpha Ryker and my pack will protect you,' I assure her.

'I don't know if I could leave all the other pack members,' she cries, 'I'd never be able to return and could never see them again.'

'At least think about it until you find the key,' I suggest. Amelia nods and leaves the cell, and retreats upstairs.

Tired, I curl up on the cold bench and hug myself to keep warm. *I'm playing hide and seek in the woods with mum. She has long brown hair and green eyes. I watch her run through the trees. 'Come on, Astrid, darling. It's your turn to find me,' she says. Closing my eyes, I count to thirty. My mum is quick on her feet and can run twice as fast as anyone I know. My mother is so strong and very kind. I admire her strengths. She is the most loving mother I could ask for. She always tells me how special I am. I never believe her. I figure mum is being biased because I'm her daughter. 'When you're eighteen, you'll believe me,' she says, smiling at me.*

Slowly, I wander through the trees, searching for her. I see rustling in the distance up ahead. 'Found you!' I shout. I run toward the rustling, only to hear a growl. I freeze in place, slowly stepping backwards in fear. Panic fills my body. I see movement in my peripheral vision. Mum has her index finger over her lips, motioning for me to keep quiet. I'm shaking with fear. Mum points behind me.

Turning around, I tiptoe into the shrubbery she points to. I lie still, flat on my tummy, with both hands over my mouth to conceal the sounds of my breathing. A vast grey wolf wanders around, sniffing. It lets out a loud growl.

For a moment, I closed my eyes. I can hear the wolf walking toward me. I open my eyes. My mother has a look of fear on her face. She slowly shakes her head and holds eye contact with me, motioning for me not to move. The big grey wolf slowly walks past me. He is ragged and worn and is even missing one of his ears. I've never seen such a ferocious animal. I tremble where I lie.

The wolf sniffs around before emitting a vicious, blood-curdling growl. I scream in fear. The wolf turns, spotting me. I quickly stand and start running. The wolf gives chase until I hear my mother yell, 'It's me you want!' The wolf stops chasing me and runs toward my mother. 'Astrid! Run!' She screams. I don't want to leave her. I run a small distance and climb a tree. My mother's body lies limp. I can see blood pooling beside her. 'Mum!' I scream at the top of my lungs, crying. The wolf circles her. The wolf has blood on his face from my mother's wounds.

My Dad is yelling in the distance, 'Astrid!'

'Daddy!' I scream. The wolf looks right at me. I'm terrified. He walks toward me like I'm his prey until the sound of a gunshot rings out. Bang! The wolf retreats.

'Astrid?' My Dad calls out again, this time much closer. Another shot rings out. Bang!

'Dad! Over here!' I scream. The wolf turns and runs, knowing Dad is approaching. When the wolf is gone, I climb down the tree.

'Astrid! What's wrong? I heard your screams. Where is your mother?' he asks, in a panic.

'W-wolf... wolf... wolf...,' I cry, shaking in fear and sobbing.

'A wolf?' Dad asks. I point in mum's direction.

'The wolf got her, Dad,' I say, bursting into tears.

Dad's face pales. He grabs my hand, and we wonder cautiously toward my mother's body. Dad drops to his knees, lifts her head to his chest, and cries. 'My love! My beautiful love!' He cries. I crawl over to my mother, take her hand, hold it up to my face and cry. We stay like this for a while until Dad says something.

'Astrid, you need to tell me exactly what happened,' he says firmly.

'We were playing hide and seek. It was my turn to find her. I thought I had found her, but it wasn't her. It was a wolf. He growled and came out from behind the trees. Mum wanted me to hide in the shrubs. Even though I was so scared, I stayed as still as possible, but the wolf came close and scared me again with an angry, loud growl. I didn't mean to scream, Daddy. The wolf chased me, and I ran. Mum yelled out at the wolf. She said it was her the wolf wanted. She screamed for me to keep running. When I turned, the wolf was hurting her. So, I ran to that tree and climbed it. Then I screamed, and you came here,' I say, crying. I look at Dad. I've never seen him look at me that way before. It's a look of pure hatred.

'Daddy?' I say, crying. Dad grabs me by the hair and drags me back toward our house.

'Daddy, Daddy. What are you doing? Why are you hurting me?' I yell.

'It's your fault she is dead! It's your fault the wolf killed her! If you listened to her, obeyed her and stayed still, she would still be alive,' he yells. 'Daddy, please! I didn't mean to kill her! Please! I didn't mean to!' I'm dragged upstairs to my room and thrown inside. My Dad slams my door closed, and I hear a key locking the door for the first time.

'Mum!' I scream, sitting up drenched in sweat. I look around the cell and let my eyes adjust. My breathing is heavy, and my heart races with panic. It was just a dream, the same dream I always have. Huddled in the corner of the dirty cell, I rest my chin on my knees. I jerk my head up when I feel a presence.

'Who's there?' I ask, sniffling. Footsteps come closer. Alpha Zenith has a grin on his face. I glare at him.

'What do you want?' I yell.

'You know very well what I want,' he snaps back.

'I'm not letting James mark me. I sure as hell won't be his mate!' I yell. His grin changes into a glare.

'Do you know you were screaming out for your mother before you woke?' He says. I look at the ground.

'What happened to her?' He asks.

'None of your damn business!' I yell.

'What if I told you I already know?' He says, grinning again. I look at him, confused.

'What would you say if I said I knew your mother?' He asks.

'I don't believe you,' I say, looking away again.

He laughs, drags an old rickety chair in front of my cell door, and sits.

'Well, aren't you in for a big surprise?' He says with a smirk and crosses his arms.

Jazz Ford

CHAPTER 17

Alpha Zenith

'I'm going to tell you a story, Astrid. And you're going to listen to every word,' he says. I glare at him but give him my full attention because I know he can make me listen if he has to, and I've been through enough.

'Twenty-two years ago, Moonstone Crest was the strongest pack around. They hosted an annual mating ceremony, where packs would be invited from around the world to potentially find their mates.'

'Unexpectedly, my pack, Shady Crest, had been invited. Unfortunately, my father was the Alpha and did not get along with the Alpha of Moonstone Crest. My father was willing to put his hatred for Alpha Bane aside, though, as he hoped I'd find my mate there. I could finally take over as Alpha if I did.'

'We attended the mating ceremony, and it was a spectacular event. However, not long after arriving, I was hit with an alluring scent of vanilla and honey. I followed the scent to no avail. I didn't understand why my mate's scent kept disappearing. Surely, she could smell my scent too, which should make her want to come to me.'

'Confused, I told my father I could smell my mate but couldn't find her. We spent most of the night searching for her. The scent finally led me to the front of the Moonstone Crest packhouse. I looked up to see the most beautiful girl I had ever seen looking out the window. She is frightened when she sees me. 'Please! Wait!' I yell as she backs away from the window. She slowly re-approaches the windowsill, and we stare into each other's eyes.

The world vanishes. It's as though only she and I exist. Nothing else matters. 'Mate', we both say. Our eyes turn black, then silver for a moment, and then they return to our standard colours. 'Please come down, so we can meet properly,' I say, smiling. She shakes her head no. 'I'm sorry, I can't,' she says in her sweet voice. I give her a confused look. 'But we're mates! Surely you can come down so we can talk? And maybe have a dance?'

'Her beautiful green eyes were like emeralds, and her long brown hair blows in the wind. 'You don't understand. Mate-bond or not, my father would never let me be with the future Alpha of Shady Crest.' She cries.

'Confused with her words, I ask her, what's wrong with being the future Luna of Shady Crest? She tells me: 'your father has tarnished the pack's name with his wicked ways and treatment of his pack. He kidnaps and hunts humans for sport,' she says.'

'Why should my father's ways affect us?' I ask, becoming angry. 'My father will make me reject you regardless of how good or bad your heart is. I'm sorry,' she explains tearfully.'

'We can figure this out, my love! But, please, just come down. I will speak to your father and tell him and show him I will treat you like a Queen,' I beg her. She continues to wipe tears from her face and shake her head.

'If you won't come down here, then I will have to come up there!' I tell her, breaking the front door down. I run upstairs and push her bedroom door open. I march over to her, but she has so much sadness in her eyes.'

'Leaning over her, I hold her chin in my hand. The chemistry between us is magical. I lean my head down to brush my lips against hers. I cup her face in my hands, and she places her hands on my chest.'

'Our lips meld together with intense passion. It feels so right and so good. Our lips finally part, and she bursts into tears. 'My sweet love, who is your father?' I ask. She looks away. 'Alpha Bane of Moonstone Crest,' she whispers.'

'In shock, I take a step back. 'You're Alyssa, the daughter of Alpha Bane?' I say. She looks up into my eyes and nods. I pull her into my chest, letting her cry. I stroke her hair to comfort her.'

'Our fathers are the greatest of enemies. There has to be a way for us to be together,' I say. 'Come, Alyssa, take my hand. Let us go to the dance. If everyone sees us happy together, maybe our fathers will approve of us. We must try at least, my love,' I say.'

'Alyssa nods. We smile at each other and walk hand in hand to the dance. All eyes are on us, in shock, as we walk in. Everyone stares, not expecting *us* to be matched by the Moon Goddess. We dance among the others as sparks fly between us. Alyssa's smile brightens the room. We stare lovingly into each other's eyes.'

'What is the meaning of this? Get away from my daughter now!' Alpha Bane yells across the room. Everyone gasps and stands aside to let Alpha Bane through. Alyssa clings to my coat and looks up at me. Her beautiful green eyes well with tears.'

'Alpha Bane, it's a pleasure to meet you,' I say, most respectfully, bowing my head. 'Alyssa, come here now!' He snaps. 'Dad, it's okay. Zenith is my mate,' she says with a nervous smile for her dad.'

'Alpha Bane's face pales instantly. 'No. The Moon Goddess would not be so cruel to mate my precious daughter with the lowest pack. You're the most hated pack in the world,' he yells.'

'I stiffen at his words. 'Alpha Bane, please. I can assure you Alyssa is my mate, and I'm so honoured to accept her as my mate. I know you and my father don't see eye to eye, but—' I'm interrupted.'

'See eye to eye? Your father murders humans for fun! The man beats his pack members. He is the only Alpha known to keep pack members as slaves. He is sick and twisted,' Alpha Bane yells.'

'Enough!' My Dad yells and steps forward out of the crowd. He looks at Alyssa, clinging to me with tears in her eyes, with my arm around her waist, clasping her tight. My Dad chuckles at the situation.'

'Who would have thought? My son, blessed with your daughter,' he chuckles. 'The Moon Goddess must surely hate you, Alpha Bane, to make you share grand-pups with me!' Dad chuckles.'

'Dad. This mateship is a blessing for Alyssa and me. So, you need to keep your taunts to yourself!' I yell at him. My

Dad growls at me for disrespecting him in front of all the packs.'

'Alyssa! You are to reject Zenith right now!' Alpha Bane orders. Alyssa and I both flinch at his demand. We stare into each other's eyes. I shake my head no. I plead with Alyssa not to do it.'

'She doesn't want to reject me. She wants to accept me. 'Now!' Alpha Bane yells, making her jump. 'You wouldn't dare make her reject my son!' My father yells at Alpha Bane. Alpha Bane grabs Alyssa by the wrist and pulls her to him. 'Alyssa, you listen to me now. You deserve better. You deserve to be with the best Alpha out there! Do you think you will have a happy life in that packhouse?' He yells.'

'He forcefully turns Alyssa around by her arms. 'Do it now, or everyone will know you as a traitor to this family. Do you want your mother living with that reputation?' Alyssa is crying. She shakes her head no.'

'Forgive me, Zenith. Please forgive me. I, Alyssa Moonstone, reject you, future Alpha Zenith of Shady Crest as my mate.' I'm crippled with severe pain in my chest. It feels like she has ripped my heart out. I see Alyssa in the same pain, gripping her chest. Everyone gasps and watches on in horror. Rejecting mates is extremely rare. Most would never witness a rejection in their lifetime.'

'The mating ceremony is over! Everyone, go home!' Alpha Bane yells. He still has his hands around Alyssa. He is pulling her away toward the packhouse. I want to run to her, but my father grabs me and holds me back.'

'You will pay for this, Alpha Bane! I swear to the Moon Goddess, you will pay!' I yell.'

'Four months pass. My father and I organise our warriors to wipe out the Moonstone pack so I can free Alyssa and bring her home with me where she belongs. We have it all planned out. First, we would trespass onto Moonstone Crest the night of Alpha Bane's birthday celebrations, discreetly killing guards and warriors one by one. The celebrations would be in the great hall where the mating ceremony is held. Then, once I find Alyssa, I will lure her away. My warriors would then close all the doors, barricading them in, pour fuel outside the hall, block the doors, and set the building on fire.'

Jazz Ford

CHAPTER 18

Alpha Zenith

'The moment I see Alyssa, my heart races. I watch her for a while and notice she doesn't seem sad or depressed. At least not in the way I have been since I've been away from her. She laughs and dances with everyone. She even clings to her dad's arm, kissing him on his cheek. *I don't understand. Why isn't she upset or angry at him? Why does she look so happy?* I thought there had to be a good explanation.'

'Alyssa walks over to the food table, plucks some grapes and strawberries from a fruit bowl, and eats them. 'Alyssa', I whisper. She stops herself from reaching for another strawberry and looks around. 'Alyssa', I whisper again.'

'She looks around to see me hiding in the garden. Her lips part as she lets out a small gasp. She is shocked to see me. She scans her surroundings to see if anyone is watching her and then looks back at me. I gesture for her to walk over to me. She is very hesitant and is debating whether or not to approach me.'

'She bites her lip and gives me a small nod to say she will come to me. Then, she looks around again and discreetly leaves the hall. My warriors watch me from their hiding spots, waiting for the signal to shut and seal the doors to set the hall alight.'

'As soon as Alyssa approaches, I pull her into my chest and hold her tight. Although I can't feel the sparks or the bond because of the rejection, I don't mind. The Moon Goddess gave her to me, and I knew I would always love her, no matter what.'

'Zenith, what are you doing here?' She asks, pushing me away.

'I'm here to save you. I will take you away from here to be my mate and Luna.' I smile. Alyssa takes a step back.

'Zenith... I don't know what to say. I don't know how to tell you...' she says with sadness.'

'You don't have to thank me, Alyssa. We can be together! Your father can never stop us this way,' I say, smiling down at her. She looks at me, confused. 'Zenith, I rejected you. We can't be together. I need you to understand that. I'm to be mated with Alpha Axton from the Justice pack in a few days,' she says. Angry at her words, I let out a growl. 'No, mate of mine will be mated to another wolf.' My wolf is angry and is trying to shift. My eyes are black from her words.'

'Zenith, we no longer have the bond. It would be best if you moved on for your family's and your sake. I like Alpha Axton. My father thinks they will be the next strongest pack. My family wants me to be with him. I also want to be with Alpha Axton,' she says.'

'No!' I say firmly. Alyssa flinches and stares into my wolf's eyes. She steps backwards, and her eyes water. I can sense she is about to run. I signal the warriors to shut and seal the doors. But before she can run, I throw her over my shoulder. 'You're coming home with me where you belong!' I say. Screams erupt from the hall. Pack members bang on the doors in need of escape.'

'Alyssa screams in horror when she realises what I'm doing. She kicks and punches with all her might until I drop her to the ground. She tries to run to the hall to open the door to free everyone. Grabbing her again, I hold her tightly in my arms. I sit away from the hall but close enough to feel the fire radiating from the flames. I hold her in my lap and stroke her hair. She cries and screams. I tell her we can be together, and I'll make a new hall for her at Shady Crest.'

'The screams stop, and the hall collapses—smoke billows around us. My father approaches, smiles, and looks down at Alyssa, who is distressed. 'Welcome to the family, sweetheart,' Dad says. Alyssa spits at him. He slaps her across the face. I let go of Alyssa and stand. 'Never slap my mate!' I yell at him. He smirks and looks past my shoulder. Alyssa stands there shaking in anger. 'You! You killed my father!' She screams, 'You murdered my entire pack!'

'She punches my chest over and over in anger. 'I hate you! I hate you! I hate you!' She screams. 'My father was only trying to protect me from men like your father!' She yells. 'I'm not like my father,' I say, in shock.'

'You just let my father and an innocent pack burn! Children! Mothers! Fathers! Brothers! Sisters! You murdered them all! You are worse than your father!' She screams. My heart sinks at the truth in her words.'

'Alyssa. It's not meant to be like this,' I say. 'I will never be your mate, Zenith. Not now, never. You've murdered my family and my pack! I'm going to leave and be with Alpha Axton,' She yells, crying.'

'She shifts into her wolf and runs to the woods. Her wolf is enormous, with pure white, long fur—almost the size of an Alpha wolf. Moonstone Crest is the only pack with pure white wolves. They're descendants of the Moon Goddess.'

'I'm angry, and I chase after her. 'I will find you, Alyssa, and you will be my mate! Or you can choose to die!' I yell before shifting into my wolf. Her wolf is faster than mine. I can't catch her. I let out a long, loud, heartbroken howl and returned to the warriors and my father, whom I'm furious with. It was his idea to kill the entire pack. I should not have listened to him. My Dad laughs. I'm growling and snapping at him.'

'Wanting justice, I challenge him. The warriors gasp, knowing a challenge is a fight to the death. My Dad accepts the challenge and shifts into his wolf. Being Alpha, he is larger than my wolf, but his age is his weakness and my advantage.'

'Lunging at my father, we roll, taking swipes at each other and biting into each other's flesh as soon as there is an opportunity to do so. Blood splatters onto the warriors as they watch on. Finally, I bite my father's throat and rip his head off.'

'I immediately grow larger and come into my power, letting out a loud howl to announce myself as the new Alpha. I have many wounds. My Dad had bitten my ear off during the fight. I shift back into human form, with my ear mostly gone. I return to the packhouse as the new Alpha.'

'My search for Alyssa and her pack spans months and then years. In the meantime, I accept Alice as my chosen mate. She has a crush on me. We eventually have a daughter Vanessa, and two twin sons: James followed by John.'

'I'm a ruthless Alpha and often lose my temper. I never stop searching for Alyssa. Years later, I discovered the Justice pack had been wiped out, and only Alyssa escaped. She was with child, carrying Alpha Axton's baby. After being in two packs that were both wiped out, she wants to live amongst humans. She can't bear the thought of raising her baby in the werewolf world.'

'She moves to the city, where she meets a human who falls deeply in love with her. They buy a house together near the woods. She loves nature, and being a wolf, she shifts secretly and goes for runs in the woods. Her human lover doesn't know what she and the baby truly are. He loves her so much, and her daughter knows only him as her dad. She wants her daughter to have a wolf-free life for as long as possible and protect her from the danger and brutality of the werewolf world. Once her daughter turns eighteen, shifting into a wolf is inevitable. Just before her eighteenth birthday, Alyssa intends to tell her about her wolf DNA.

'When her daughter is around seven, and my sons are not much older, I find out where they live. The house emits sweet giggles. I watch and wait in the woods until I hear Alyssa's voice. 'Come on, Astrid, darling. It's your turn to find me!' Although I can't see you, I know you're hiding somewhere. Sniffing around, I catch your scent. Maybe if I growl, I can scare you into moving, and it works. I knew chasing you would make her come out. 'It's me you want, she yells. She knew it was me. She knew I would never stop looking for her.'

'I run toward her and lunge at her. My teeth sink into her neck while I shake her around like a rag doll, and the colour fades from her face, and she becomes lifeless. Once I know, she is dead. I also consider killing you in the tree until I hear the gunshots. I have achieved my goal, killing your mother for leaving me for Alpha Axton.'

'I decide to monitor you over the years. I know your stepfather isn't treating you well. It makes me happy knowing it would have made your mother miserable.'

'My pack runs differently from other packs. I don't want to go along with the whole fated-mate shindig. Instead, I decide to match people with mates who increase the pack's strength. Vanessa, pretending to be a victim, goes to Shadow Crest with the mission to mark and mate Ryker, one of the strongest alphas around other than myself, of course. Alice is stubborn, though, and doesn't want to leave Vanessa. So, I send them both and keep in contact with them daily. Alice spends the odd night here, with Shadow Crest none-the-wiser.'

'Knowing you are of Moonstone Crest and Justice pack DNA means you are a powerful wolf with rare genes and likely a pure white wolf who would breed strong pups with my son. Amelia is an Alpha's daughter too, mixed with a secret gene that only her family and I know about, who, with a substantial dowry, handed her over to be mated with John.'

'Love no longer matters. It doesn't matter if the Moon Goddess gives you a mate. There is always a chance you'll be rejected and left for someone else, regardless of how strong the bond is! I learned power is stronger than love that night.'

'That's what I taught my pack: it's less heart-breaking to choose a mate who will benefit you and the pack, and a fated mate's rejection is gut-wrenching.'

'My kids agreed. I killed the boy's fated mates. They were weak Omegas. Can you believe that? Omegas matched to future alphas! I killed Vanessa's mate, too. He was the weakest wolf I had ever seen: more mutt than wolf. And now, here you are, the day before your eighteenth birthday, about to be marked with my eldest son. How did it go? Oh, yes. 'Welcome to the family, sweetheart,' Alpha Zenith says with a sadistic smile.

CHAPTER 19

Astrid

In utter shock, I can't believe what Alpha Zenith has just told me. He is my mother's true mate and murderer. I stand, run to the cell door, and shake the bars with fury full of anger.

'You killed my mother! You killed her!' I yell. Alpha Zenith smiles.

'Yes, I killed her! After everything I did for her! I gave her a chance to reunite with me, and she threw it away like I was nothing, like I wasn't even worth the risk!' He yells.

'You killed her whole family! You murdered them all in cold blood! She didn't want to be with a monster!' I yell. The look on Alpha Zenith's face changes from a smile to aggression. He unlocks the cell door and grabs me by the throat, holding me against the cold stone wall.

'What did you call me?' He growls, squeezing my throat tighter. I try to loosen his hands from my throat. I can't breathe. Black dots appear in my vision, and he loosens his grip and speaks.

'Call me a monster again, Astrid,' he warns. Boring his eyes with mine, I know he will kill me if I call him anything again. I shake my head in defeat.

'That's what I thought,' he says, dropping me to the ground. Tears stain my face, and I'm gasping for oxygen.

'Pathetic!' He says, staring down at me, before smirking and walking away.

I feel like I will explode. A cocktail of emotions swarms through me with all this new information about my mother, father and the pack I come from. I stand, grab the sides of my head, and let out the loudest, most frustrated scream. James comes running down the stairs.

'Astrid! What's wrong?' He asks, concerned.

'What's wrong? What's wrong?' I repeat, in disbelief, at his dumb question. 'I'm locked in a cold, dirty cell, forced to be your mate! Your father murdered my mother! He wiped out her whole pack! I want to be with Ryker, where I am supposed to be! And you dare to ask me what is wrong?' I yell. James looks away.

'Did you know your father killed my mother? Did you know he murdered an entire pack?' I yell. James looks at me in silence for a moment.

'Yes, I know. The whole pack knows. Most pack members are afraid to disobey him. They know he'll kill them in the blink of an eye. They all know you're Alyssa Moonstone's daughter, the only werewolf left from Moonstone Crest. Why do you think everyone was so excited to meet you when you arrived?' He asks.

'I hate you,' I say in a low voice. James stiffens and glares at me.

'Look, I need to help Dad in the office today. I will come to see you when I return,' he says.

'I'd prefer you never come near me again,' I retort.

James crosses his arms in anger and goes upstairs. Hours pass. I'm guessing it's late afternoon. It's hard to tell with no windows down here. *I wonder if Amelia had any luck finding the cell key.* For self-entertainment, I throw small stones between the cell door bars, missing half the time.

Suddenly, I hear yelling and cries. Light appears on the stairs as the door opens. Someone shoves Amelia down the stairs. She cries out as she stumbles and falls.

'Please, John, I'm sorry!' She says.

'Don't waste your apologies on me! Save them for the Alpha!' John yells. He stomps heavily across the stone floor, grabbing Amelia by the hair and dragging her into the cell next to mine. He throws her in and slams the cell door shut.

'Amelia!' I shout. We look at each other. Her eyes are red and puffy from crying. She has a few minor bruises on her neck.

'Astrid, I'm sorry,' she cries, looking away.

'I caught my little mate, Amelia here, rummaging through my father's things, and forced her to confess what she was looking for,' John says, smirking.

'You were supposed to be at work today!' Amelia yells at John.

'I was but came home early. We had some issues with Ryker from Shadow Crest, which we had to take care of. So dad sent me home to prepare the warriors. In case Ryker tries to break in and rescue his dear little Astrid,' John says.

'Ryker is looking for me?' I ask excitedly. *How did Ryker know to go to Zenith Creations? He must have found the business card. I left it in my room.*

'Don't get too excited sweet cheeks,' John says. 'His beta, Seth and others found your scent in the city but lost the trail. Seth broke into our underground car park after picking up your scent again. Pack warriors patrol at night. We caught Seth, as you know, and he has been in the basement since. We only let him out to interrogate and rough him up,' John laughs.

'Wait! That guy you beat up the other day was Seth?' I ask, in shock.

'Sure was,' he chuckles.

'You're a bastard! You know that, John?' I yelled, glaring at him.

'Yep. I know it, and I like it,' John laughs.

'What has Alpha Zenith told Ryker?' I ask, needing more information.

'Dad told him you begged him for temp work, to skip town, so we gave you work for a few days, paid you cash, and then you left.' he smiles.

'Did he believe it?' I ask.

'I don't know. Hence, James and I came back to the house to prepare, just in case he trespassed and searched for you and Seth. Anyway, I'm sure your soon-to-be mate, James, will come to see you shortly. Alpha Zenith should be back soon, too. I'm interested to see what Amelia's punishment is for trying to help you escape,' he says with a smirk.

John leaves Amelia and me, and I crawl over to her on my hands and knees on the stone floor and reach out to her. She is shaking and petrified, as am I.

'Amelia, look at me,' I whisper. Amelia slowly looks up at me with her pretty brown eyes.

'I won't let anything happen to you, okay?' I promise.

'Astrid, there is nothing you can do,' she says, wiping tears from her face.

'Ryker will save us. He is coming to save me. I just know it, and you will come home with us!' I say reassuringly.

'I hope you're right,' she sobs.

Moments later, Alpha Zenith enters the cells, dragging Seth down the stairs. A calico bag is over his head, and he isn't moving. Seth's wrists are tied together with rope.

'Seth!' I yell.

'Yell all you want. I knocked Seth out good!' Alpha Zenith laughs as he drags Seth to a cell opposite mine and throws him into the cell like a bag of potatoes.

'Why the hell are you in here, Amelia?' He growls. Amelia bursts into tears, frightened.

'Ah, fuck it. I've got more important shit to deal with right now,' Alpha Zenith snaps, stomping off.

Amelia and I stay huddled up, despite the bars between us. It must be nightfall when James comes down the steps.

He unlocks my cell door, not saying a word, and gazes at me the whole time. Then, he pulls me away from Amelia.

'Don't touch me! Get your hands off me!' I yell, trying to slap his face. He pins my wrists between us, holding them tightly.

'I wish I could mark you right now, Astrid,' he whispers. Shuddering at his words, I recoil from him.

'I look forward to your first shift tomorrow night. Ever since Ryker showed up looking for you, I haven't been able to stop thinking of you. The thought of him taking you from me is not good,' he says.

'I belong with Alpha Ryker, not you! You'll be sorry when he finds me!' I yell. James glares and pushes me harshly against the bars.

'You are mine! And I'll claim you as mine after your first shift. I'll ensure you're bearing my pups by the night's end!' He growls.

'I will never mate with you. I would rather die than bear your pups!' I yell. James strikes my face, and I fall to the ground.

'Astrid!' Amelia cries out. James storms out of the cell, locking it behind him.

'I'm okay. I'm sorry you had to see that,' I say.

'Astrid, we need to get out of here!' Amelia cries.

'I know,' I say, looking away. Seth sits up.

'Seth! Seth!' He raises his wrists to his face to take the calico bag off his head. He spends a few moments squinting before his eyes adjust.

'Astrid?' He wonders.

'Yes, it's me! Seth - I'm so glad you're awake. I was so worried!'

'Where are we?' He is dizzy and disoriented.

'We're in the cells underneath the Shady Crest packhouse.'

'Who is that?' He asks, nodding to the cell next to mine.

'Amelia. She tried to help me escape, but she got caught. She is John's chosen mate,' I explain.

'Why would anyone have a chosen mate?' He asks.

'Alpha Zenith doesn't want his children or pack members to be with their true mates. So, he killed Vanessa, James' and John's mates. Alpha Zenith says they were weak omegas. He wants only high-ranking, powerful werewolves to produce pups with his kids. He wants them to breed stronger wolf pups to make the pack stronger. Amelia is the daughter of an alpha from another pack. He bought her to breed with John. He is trying to force me to mate with James after my first shift tomorrow night,' I explain.

The look on Seth's face says it all.

'Astrid, you are Alpha Ryker's mate! You are my Luna! You can't mate with James!' He yells.

'We need to think of a way to escape before I shift. Otherwise, we have to hope Ryker saves us,' I say. Seth and Amelia nod in agreement. We spend the rest of the evening devising a plan but come up with nothing. Amelia tried to dig her way out, only to find disappointment and stone. Seth tried to bend the cell bars, to no avail. While I attempted to pick the lock with a bobby pin, I took from Amelia's hair. We sit and stare at each other in defeat.

'We can only hope that Ryker saves us,' Seth says in dismay.

Jazz Ford

CHAPTER 20

Alpha Ryker

We arrive in the city, park outside Zenith Creations, enter the facility, and find an elevator. The elevator door dings and opens. We step out and spot a large door and enter. It's quite a modern, sleek waiting room. It even has a water feature on one wall. I approach the large desk to see a blonde receptionist on the phone. Leaning on the desk, I tap my fingers impatiently. The receptionist raises a perfectly shaped brow at me. I take the phone from her and throw it behind her.

'Excuse me!' She says, 'That was a significant client on the phone!' She yells.

'I don't give a shit who was on the phone. Where's Zenith? I want to speak with him immediately!' I yell. She picks up a phone and presses a button.

'There is a vulgar man here, with two other men wanting to speak with you immediately,' she says. She covers the mic on the phone with her nail-polished hand.

'What is your name?' She asks.

'Alpha Ryker,' I snap.

'Alpha Ryker, sir. Yes, okay. I will send them in,' she tells Alpha Zenith. She puts the phone down and stands. 'Follow me, please,' she says.

We're escorted to the middle door a few metres behind her desk. Alpha Zenith sits in an oversized chair behind a desk with two bodyguards.

'Alpha Ryker! What a surprise to see you here. Please, sit,' he says with a smile.

'No, we will stay standing. Where is she?' I ask.

'Where is who?' Zenith asks. Placing my hand in my pocket, I pull the card out and slam it onto his desk.

'My mate, Astrid. I know she is here. We can smell her scent!' Zenith pauses and stares at the business card.

'I found this card in her room after she ran,' I say.

'Yes. Astrid was here, but only for a few days. She asked

me for a few days' work to skip town. I didn't question her. She was a young girl who needed help, so I helped her and gave her a job, and she left,' Zenith explains.

'You're lying,' I yell. Zenith puts his hands in the air.

'Look, believe me, or don't believe me, I don't care. I don't know why you're bothering to find Astrid if she doesn't want to be with you. Maybe you should let her be,' he suggests.

'She only left because some of your old pack members threatened to kill her if she didn't!' I growl. Zenith has a poker face, and his two men look at each other.

'And which old members would they be?' Zenith asked.

'Alice and Vanessa. But not to worry: they're currently locked up awaiting punishment.' I notice the two men give each other another look and then glare at me.

'And what will their punishment be?' Zenith asked calmly.

'I'll have them killed and their heads ripped off for threatening my Luna and mate,' I say, lying. Zenith glares for a split second.

'I see,' he says, his fists clenched.

'I suppose you haven't seen my missing beta Seth either?' I ask, expecting another denial. I can smell Seth's scent in the room. He has been here as well.

'No, we haven't, but I will let you know if Astrid contacts me if you like?' He says. I glare at him. He is the worst liar I have ever met.

'I would appreciate that.'

'Your beta and gamma?' I ask, looking at the two men.

'These are my sons: James, the future Alpha of Shady Crest and John,' he says. James glares at me as though he despises me and wants to rip my head off. John is smirking.

'I'm sure we will see each other again soon,' I say, leaving Kane and Leon following behind. Out of the elevator, we go straight to the car.

'He is lying,' I say.

'We figured as much,' Kane says.

'I can smell Seth's scent. He has been there,' I point out.

'What's our next move?' Leon asks.

'Let's get back home and make a plan. We will need all our warriors,' I say.

We arrive at Shadow Crest a short while later.

'Leon, get the maps of Shady Crest from the library. Kane, bring Mia and Hayley here.' They both nod and leave. Leon returns a short time later with a couple of scrolls he hands me.

'Alpha Ryker!' Mia says as she enters the room, Kane and Hayley behind her.

'Please tell me you found them,' she says, hopeful. I shake my head.

'No, but I can confirm they were both at Zenith Creations. Their scents were faint but were there. Alpha Zenith denied seeing Seth but said Astrid worked for him for a few days before leaving with enough money to skip town. So, he has them. He's lying.'

We gather around the table and roll out the map showing Shady Crest.

'I think they're in his house. They're not exactly going to

let us have a look around. The only way in is if we trespass and declare war. The girls gasped.

'If we go to war, some of our pack members could die, ' Hayley grabs Kane's arm tightly.

'No one has to die,' I reassure her.

'How so?' Leon asks, confused.

'When we were in the office today, I mentioned Vanessa and Alice as the reason why Astrid fled. I told him they would be punished by death. Zenith tried to hide it, but he and his sons weren't happy about it. We need to find out why he doesn't want Alice and Vanessa harmed. Leon, take a few warriors with you and bring Alice and Vanessa here for questioning.' Leon nods and leaves the room.

Leon returns with warriors who are dragging Alice and Vanessa into the room. They sit on a chair next to each other. Alice spits at my feet as I approach.

'That isn't very nice, Alice,' I say. She lets out a deranged laugh.

'You have to tell me, what are you to, Shady Crest? What

are your rankings?' I ask. Alice glares at me, remaining silent. Vanessa stares into my eyes with sadness.

'Why couldn't you just love me as I loved you?' She cries. Kneeling in front of her, I lean in closer.

'What are you to, Alpha Zenith?' I ask, glaring at her. Vanessa recoils from me and looks away.

'You will answer me, or Mia will convince you to talk.' I motion for Mia to step forward, and she cracks her knuckles, giving Vanessa a death stare.

'I'm his daughter,' she confesses. I could have heard a pin drop.

'Vanessa!' Alice growls at her.

'You're Alpha Zenith's daughter? That makes Alice the Luna of Shady Crest! You said they abused you, that you were the pack slaves! Why did you come here if you're the Luna, and you're his daughter?' I ask, half questioning, half-wondering.

'Vanessa, keep your mouth shut!' Alice snaps.

'Leon, take Alice back to her cell,' I order. Once Alice is gone, I grab Vanessa by the chin.

'Tell me everything you know, now!' I demand.

'My father, Alpha Zenith, sent me here to become Luna and bear your pups. But unfortunately, he killed my true mate. Dad said my mate was weak, and his children would only breed with the best. Knowing you were mateless and one of the strongest alphas around, he told me to seek refuge here, with the intent of us sleeping together. The irony is, the moment I met you, I instantly had a crush on you. It was all too easy to fulfil Dad's wishes.'

'Do you know where Astrid is?' I ask. Vanessa looks away.

'Please, Vanessa, she's my mate. I love her. Tell me, and your punishment will be lenient,' I compromise.

Vanessa looks at me. My eyes are pleading with her.

'I'm only going to tell you, Ryker, because I love you, and I want you to be happy,' she says, tears rolling down her cheeks.

'She is at Shady Crest,' she confesses.

'I knew it! Seth's there too!' I growl.

'Wait! There is something you should know. My brother James plans on marking her, and sleeping with her, tomorrow night after her shift,' she says. Angry, I growl loudly at her words.

'No wonder he wanted to rip my head off when I saw him today,' I ponder.

'Kane, let's go over the map and find the best strategy to defeat Zenith and his pack. Leon, you can get the warriors prepared. Then, tomorrow evening, it's war!' I declare.

Jazz Ford

CHAPTER 21

'Happy Birthday!' Amelia says as I wake.

'Happy Birthday, Luna!' Seth cheers. I can't help but laugh.

'Who would have thought I'd be celebrating my eighteenth in a cold, dirty cell?' I chuckle. Seth and Amelia laugh. We all go silent in thought.

'Astrid?' Amelia says, concerned.

'I'm terrified. I'm meeting my wolf tonight. What if Ryker doesn't save us in time? What if James marks me?' I worry.

'Let's see if I can mind-link Alpha Ryker. James and John injected wolfsbane into me. But unfortunately, it weakened me and hindered our connection,' Seth says. We watch on as he concentrates, his eyes clouding over.

'Is it working?' I ask. Seth nods.

'I've gotten through to Alpha Ryker!' He says. I run to my cell door, hold the bars, and partially squeeze my head through them.

'Seth, tell him I'm sorry. Tell Ryker I am so sorry. I should not have left. I didn't want to leave!' I yell desperately.

'Ryker says he knows. Vanessa confessed everything. Did you know Alice poisoned him so Vanessa could mark him?' Seth says. I gasp.

'Please tell me she didn't?' I panic.

'No, Kane and Leon were there just in time. They're both in the cells now.' I relax with relief.

'He knows we're here. He will be here tonight with the warriors to free us,' he says.

'Please tell him I miss him and want to be with him.'
Seth nods.

'Um, he says he can't wait to hold you in his arms and taste your sweet lips,' Seth blushes. I giggle and blush in response.

'So, I guess we just have to wait it out until tonight,' I say.

Seth nods. I can't help but smile and hug myself. I jump up and down and do a twirl.

'I'm going to see Ryker tonight!' I say with excitement. Seth and Amelia smile at seeing me so happy and excited.

My joy is short-lived when John and James come marching down the stairs, smirking. John unlocks Amelia's door and drags her out.

'No, John. Please! Where are you taking me?' Amelia cries.

'Let her go!' I shout.

Amelia kicks and punches John.

'Stop fighting me! Alpha Zenith is ready for you. The longer you make him wait, the more lashes you'll receive!' He snaps.

'Don't you dare touch her!' I yell.

'Or what?' John yells.

'I'll rip your head off the moment I shift if you lay a finger on her!' John glares at me.

'James, I think you need to put Astrid in her place!' He warns.

John is still dragging Amelia up the stairs as she continues kicking and screaming. James enters my cell and steps forward, and I step back until I'm up against the wall with nowhere else to go. He cups my cheek with his hand.

'Tonight, we become one, and you become mine!' He whispers in my ear. Then he presses his body against mine, pinning me against the wall, and kisses my neck. I try to fight him off, but he has my hands pinned above my head.

'Get off my Luna now!' Seth growls. James pauses with annoyance and turns to Seth.

'Astrid is my Luna and my mate! I will do as I please with her, so if I were you, I would shut your trap before I come in there and rip your head off!'

James kisses my neck.

'Please! Stop!' I yell.

'Stop? We could skip waiting and mark each other now?' He says, dead serious. His fangs protrude, and he scrapes them across my shoulder. I kick him in the shin as hard as possible, and he steps back in pain. I punch him with full force, giving him a black eye.

'You little!' He snarls. I want to punch his face again, but he catches my fist in his hand, twists my arm behind my back, and locks me in a hold, so I can't move.

'You have become rather feisty, Astrid. You're not as weak as you used to be, but I can fix that!' He says, shoving me into the stone bench and locking the cell door behind me.

'Tonight, I won't be so lenient, Astrid. I suggest you get used to the idea of being my mate!' He yells as he walks upstairs.

'Astrid, are you okay?' Seth asks.

'I want to get out of here. I want to be with Ryker.'

'I know Luna, I know. I would do anything to have Mia in my arms right now, too,' he says with a sad smile. John returns downstairs in a bad mood with a food tray. His face has deep scratches.

'Where's Amelia?' I yell. He drops the food tray on the ground, not caring that half of the food rolls off into the dirt.

'The little cow went psycho, scratching the shit out of my face and ran off, but we have pack warriors everywhere if Ryker shows up. So, it's only a matter of time till she's caught and brought back here.'

'We will see you tonight for your first shift,' he says with a smile.

'Who are we?' I ask.

'Alpha Zenith, myself and your mate James,' he says. I glare at him. 'It's getting dark. I will see you soon,' he says, slinking off.

Seth and I look at each other in a comforting silence before the door creaks open and light shines in. Amelia is screaming. John drags her down the stairs and throws her into the cell next to mine.

'Amelia! Are you okay?' I ask. She nods.

'You're lucky. Ryker and his warriors have entered our territory. Otherwise, you would get far worse than lashes, Amelia!' John yells.

'Ryker is here?' I ask.

'Yes, but not to worry. I have prepared our warriors for

this,' he chuckles.

'If you hurt Ryker, I will kill you!' I scream.

'We will see,' John says, walking away.

'Amelia, what happened? Are you hurt?' I ask. I wait for Amelia to catch her breath.

'They were going to give me twenty lashes. John tried to tie me up. I scratched his face as hard and as deep as I could. Then I shifted into my wolf and ran as fast as I could. There are pack warriors spread out all over the place. I hid for as long as I could to evade them. Two of them caught me. They brought me back here to be lashed, but Alpha Zenith says it will have to wait. They have spotted alpha Ryker and his men entering our territory,' she says.

'I'm glad you aren't hurt, Amelia. I'll mind-link Alpha Ryker and let him know that Alpha Zenith is aware he's here,' Seth says. 'He says they've brought Alice and Vanessa with them, hoping to exchange them for us!'

Suddenly, a surge of pain rips through my body. I cry out in pain and roll across the cold stone floor.

'Luna!' Seth yells.

'It hurts! It hurts! Make it stop!' I cry.

'Shit! You're shifting!' Seth yells. Amelia reaches through the bars and places her hand on my back, trying to soothe me.

'I've told Alpha Ryker to hurry and that you've started shifting,' Seth says. I continue to cry out in pain.

'How long does this take?' I cry out.

'The first shift, on average, takes around half an hour,' he replies. I let out another scream as the pain surges down my spine. It is horrendous.

'Ryker!' I scream.

CHAPTER 22

Alpha Ryker

We enter Shady Crest territory right at nightfall. Vanessa and Alice walk in front of Kane with their wrists tied together while Leon leads the pack warriors. Alpha Zenith's warriors are all spread out, making them easy targets. Our arrival must have sounded an alarm. They retreat toward the packhouse.

'Alpha Zenith knows we're here,' I yell out. Seth is mind-links me: *Alpha! 'They know you're here!'*

'Good!' I say.

'Oh no!' Seth says.

'What is it?' I ask.

'It's Astrid! You need to hurry! She's shifting!' Seth says.

'Seth, tell Astrid I'm coming for her. I will be with her as soon as possible,' I say.

'Leon, Kane, we need to move fast! Astrid is shifting!' They nod. Leon and I shift into our wolves. Kane supervises Alice and Vanessa in his human form.

'We will be right behind you, Alpha!' Kane yells out.

We run until we can see the packhouse. There are hundreds of pack warriors ready and waiting for us. I shift into my human form and put my pants on. I scan the area for Alpha Zenith, keeping my eyes on him, and slowly walk toward him. Alpha Zenith paces toward me, and we come face to face. He cracks his neck from side to side. He is shirtless and ready to shift.

'Hand Astrid and Seth over now. No one has to die,' I say. Alpha Zenith laughs.

'Astrid belongs to James and this pack now.' he says.

'Kane! Bring them out!' I yell. Kane steps forward in front of our pack warriors with Alice and Vanessa. Alpha Zenith grinds his teeth and lets out a growl.

'I thought I'd bring your Luna and daughter along for the show,' I grin.

'Or we can trade. Astrid and Seth for Vanessa and Alice.' Alpha Zenith glares.

'Or I can kill you, claim your pack, and have everything I want!' He snaps.

'War it is!' I say, growling.

'War it is then!' Alpha Zenith yells as he walks back to his warriors. He shifts into an ugly, large, grey wolf. His ear is missing, and he is worn and ragged. I shift into my black wolf and let out a howl, signalling war. In wolf form, my warriors charge toward Alpha Zenith's warriors. I lose sight of him and charge toward the others, attacking us, crashing into them, and biting any area of fur exposed to me.

Two wolves run toward me and pounce. I quickly rip the throat of one out while the other bites my leg. I whimper, release the wolf I hold, and lunge at the wolf, gnashing my leg. Clawing his face, he releases me. I pounce and bite into his side, tearing a large piece of flesh from him. He retreats, yelping. I observe the two packs fighting. It isn't a pretty scene.

I shift back into human form to look for *Astrid!* I run toward the packhouse.

'Leon! Follow me!' I yell. Leon follows as we race into the packhouse. I can hear Astrid's screams beneath the floor.

'Leon, a door must lead down to the cells,' I figure.

'Astrid!' I yell, running through the house.

'Alpha! Here! I found the entrance. It smells so good, like lavender and musk,' Leon says. I push past him to time-poor for his observations and run downstairs.

Seth is in the cell on the left. A girl sits on the ground in the cell on the right. Astrid is curled up on the ground, screaming in pain.

'Astrid!' I rattle the door, but it's locked.

'Where's the key?' I ask.

'Ryker!' Astrid screams, trying to crawl toward the door. She collapses in pain and lets out a scream as a bone snaps.

'Astrid, I'm going to find the key, okay?' I run up the stairs. Leon is watching the girl in the other cell.

'Leon! What are you doing?' The girl is also gazing at Leon.

'Mate!' They both mumble in a trance.

'Leon, if you want to save your mate, I suggest we find the key!' I yell.

Leon nods, and we search in vain for the keys. Then, finally, I hear them dangling in someone's grip behind me.

'Looking for these?' A male voice behind me asks.

James dangles the keys in front of me enticingly. John is with him. I shift into my wolf as quick as James and John do. I lunge at James and bite into his chest. John bites into my ribs, and two snap in his lock-hold. Leon lunges at John, pushing him off of me. James and I fight each other, neither backing down. We are both covered in gashes. Astrid screams in pain. I lunge at James, biting down as hard as possible, ripping a sizeable chunk of flesh from his neck. Knowing he will bleed out, I finish him quickly, instantly snapping his neck. John lets out an anguished howl. Leon uses this to his advantage and rips John's stomach open.

I grab the keys back in human form and unlock Astrid's cell. I throw them over to Leon to free Seth and his mate. Our chemistry envelopes us in a sentimental degree as I hold Astrid in my arms. I gently wipe her hair from her face.

'Ryker! You're here!' She cries.

'I promised you I'd be here for your first shift,' I whisper.

I hold her tightly through her screams, feeling the discs in her spine snap as I hold her in my arms.

'You can do this. It will all be over soon. I promise,' I assure Astrid. she cries again as another bone snaps. Her muzzle develops, and her fangs protrude from her top jaw. Glossy white fur clothes her body, tearing off her skirt and blouse. Her last scream becomes a majestic howl.

'Astrid!' She tries to stand on all fours and struggles with her balance.

'Whoa!' Seth and Leon say, amazed. 'She's a pure white wolf!' Seth adds.

Unsteady on her feet. I help her balance.

'Steady now, nice and slowly. I have you.'

She is beautiful: the most beautiful wolf I have ever seen. She is so large, similar to me in size.

'Pure white wolves are only from—'

'Moonstone Crest. Astrid is the last of her pack. Her mother, Alyssa, was a future Luna, and her father was Alpha Axton,' she explains.

'How do you know?' I ask. She is holding Leon's hand tightly. Leon has his other arm around her waist and the biggest grin on his youthful face.

'Alpha Zenith is Alyssa's true mate,' she explains. We all freeze as Astrid growls and yaps.

'It's okay, Astrid,' I say. I kneel so she can lick my face. She is like a gigantic marshmallow: she is so soft and squishy when I wrap my arms around her. She tries to play fight with me, nipping at my ankles and rolling onto her back in my lap.

'I'm excited too. You're the most beautiful wolf I have ever seen.' I smile.

'Seth, see how our warriors are going. We need to defeat Alpha Zenith.'

Astrid lets out an angry growl at his name.

'I know. Try to shift back into human form. I promise shifting back doesn't hurt at all. It will only take a moment when you shift again, and it will be less painful,' I explain.

'I'm going to fight. Amelia, stay here till the fight is over,' Leon says.

'No!' Amelia shouts. 'I'm going to fight too!' She says, ripping off her clothes and shifting into her wolf with Leon. They leave the cell. It's the first time Astrid and I have been alone since she left. My eyes well with tears as I adore the love of my life and her sweet, fluffy face.

CHAPTER 23

Astrid

Focusing, like Ryker told me to. My body shifts back into human form. I open my eyes to see myself lying in Ryker's arms. I lock eyes with him, but this time, I see him through my wolf's eyes. 'Mate!' I say, and the world around me disappears. I feel a magnetic rush of endorphins and dopamine sweep through me—the attraction and lust I have for Ryker increase dramatically. I want to touch him, hold him, mark him and tell the world he is 'mine'. My arms wrap around his neck.

'Ryker, I missed you so much! I'm so sorry for leaving.'

He wraps his warm, masculine arms around my waist and presses me to his chest. He cups my face in his hands.

'It's okay, babe. I know you didn't want to leave. I'm here now, and that's all that matters.' We stare into each other's eyes, and our mouths smash together. My body ignites with the intensity of our passionate kiss. It sends overwhelming, hot shivers down my spine. We eventually part from the kiss and pant.

Ryker lets out a little growl and nips at my neck.

'As much as I want to stay like this forever, we need to destroy Alpha Zenith.' He brings me back to reality with his words. I stand up quickly, and my eyes change into my wolf's.

'Alpha Zenith is mine to kill!' I growl, instantly shifting.

Ryker shifts, and we're almost the same size. I'm only slightly smaller. We let out a loud, majestic howl in unison, warning Alpha Zenith that we are coming for him!

Bolting out of the cell, up the stairs and out of the packhouse, I see we have a lot of badly injured warriors. There are wounded wolves everywhere and many dead warriors and pack members from Shady Crest. Sprinting around for Alpha Zenith, I catch his scent. I follow it away from the battle through the long grass and creep through the trees. I can tell he is close. Ryker isn't far behind me, watching my back.

Hearing a ferocious growl on my right, I see Alpha Zenith lunging toward me in his wolf form. We roll a few metres, with Alpha Zenith pinning me down. My hind claws tear into his stomach. He emits a whimper and claws into my chest. I roll out from underneath him, then leap onto him, ferociously biting the back of his neck, and tear a piece of flesh off him. He howls in pain and then falls backward, almost crushing me beneath him.

Unable to move from under him, I rip into his ribs and hear bones breaking. He rolls off me, and we snap and snarl at each other, blood dripping from our muzzles. Alpha Zenith's neck is exposed briefly, so I lunge forward, biting as hard as possible. I Remember how he bit my mother's neck and shook her around like a rag doll. I show no mercy. Adrenaline rushes through me. Blood spurts everywhere, and I shake him around feverishly. I know he is dead, but I don't let go. Increased strength surges through me as my wolf grows larger. Having Killed Alpha

Zenith, I now have the power of an alpha, and his pack members belong to me. I'm not finished with him yet, and I release all my anger by ripping more flesh off him.

'Astrid! Enough! He's dead!' Ryker says, slowly approaching me. I let out another growl, warning Ryker to back off. He freezes on the spot, shocked by my response.

'Astrid, you killed him. You can let him go now. It's over,' he says.

So much anger is boiling up inside of me. Alpha *Zenith killed my mother! He murdered my whole family and pack in Moonstone Crest! His death hasn't satisfied me. It isn't enough compensation for what he has done.* I growl ferociously, still tearing his flesh off in strips. Masculine arms instantly wrap around me.

'Astrid! You need to stop! You need to shift into your human form. This isn't you, Astrid. Don't be the monster he is. Please! I'm begging you!' He pleads. I cringe at his words. *What am I doing? He killed my mother. I got my vengeance by killing him. But I continue to rip him apart like a monster violently.* Finally, I let go of his body. Ryker can see the pain in my face. In my dazed reverie, I tumble into his lap. I'm severely injured and have lost too much blood from my wounds. I must have blacked out because I opened my eyes to stare into Ryker's smooth jawline. He carries me bridal-style towards our pack members. Shady Crest pack members felt Alpha Zenith's death immediately and ceased fighting.

Approaching Shady Crest, the pack members see us, fall to their knees and bow their heads.

'Why are they bowing for us?' I ask Ryker.

'The moment you kill an Alpha, his pack becomes your pack,' he explains.

'But I'm not officially part of a pack yet,' I say, confused. Ryker looks at me passionately.

'All you have to do is accept me as your mate, Astrid. And take your place by my side as my equal and Luna,' he smiles. I cup his face in my hands as he cradles me.

'I, Astrid Moonstone, accept you, Alpha Ryker of Shadow Crest, as my mate and your Luna.' Ryker stares into my eyes. He is fending off tears of happiness with my words.

A strange warmth courses through my body. I feel an immediate sense of power and authority. *'Astrid, you have made me the happiest Alpha in the world,'* Ryker says, mind-linking me for the very first time. I freeze at his voice in my head.

'I just heard you. In my head. Is that the mind-link?' I ask excitedly.

'Yes, think of me in your mind. I will hear your voice in my head,' he says.

'Okay. *Ryker, if we didn't have hundreds of werewolves staring at us, I would kiss you passionately.'* Ryker lets out a chuckle.

I'm sure they wouldn't mind a show, he says mischievously.

'Ryker!' I say, slapping his chest playfully.

'I'm only joking, babe,' he says, kissing my forehead.

Amelia and Leon run up to us, holding hands. Amelia is blushing and smiling. I smile back at her, happy she has found her destined mate, who has accepted her unconditionally.

'So, Amelia and Leon, hey?' I say, smiling. 'So, what happens now?' I ask Ryker.

'Now we tend to the injured. First, we will use the Shady Crest packhouse for all the wounded. After that, the warriors will bury the dead, and we'll return to Shadow Crest. Pack members from here are welcome to come with us. Or they can stay here and resume their lives, but this land is now our territory,' he explains.

Doing my best, I help tend to the injured. Everyone calls me Luna. It's foreign to me, but I figure I'll get used to it.

'How are you feeling now?' Ryker asks, looking me up and down.

'I'm completely healed from all the injuries I received. I can't believe how quick I heal now,' I smile.

'You will always heal quickly now that you have your wolf,' he smiles. 'I think it's time we all go home.' We hold hands, keeping our eyes only on each other. Everyone else is ready to leave to go home.

'Ryker? I was wondering if we could catch up with everyone later? My wolf is begging to be let out, and I thought we could go for a run together?'

'I'd like that very much,' he smiles and kisses me passionately.

'Ready to go, Alpha and Luna?' Seth asks. Our eyes remain locked on each other. Without turning around to look at Seth, Ryker waves his hand.

'You all go home. We will catch up later,' Ryker says. Seth smiles and nods, leading everyone back to Shadow Crest. I pull my dress off and shift into my large white wolf. Ryker shifts, and I bolt toward him. We play-fight a little. I nip at his ankles and neck. He purposely falls over, feigning weakness and whimpers. I haven't had the strength to knock him to the ground. It is charming to watch; playing with his wolf is a gratifying experience.

We race through the woods to see who's faster. Our speeds aren't very different. The full moon is out in full view. We sit on a cliff edge near the packhouse and let out majestic, powerful howls together.

The pack members respond to us, howling together with joy and enthusiasm. Ryker's wolf sits beside me, resting his head on mine. He gives me a nip and a nuzzle every so often. We return to the packhouse when everyone is asleep and shift into our human forms. Before entering the front door, Ryker scoops me up and carries me upstairs to bed.

Jazz Ford

CHAPTER 24

Giggling and blushing as Ryker nips my ear playfully, I let out a slight growl. He puts me on the bed and crawls toward me, kissing me passionately.

'I love you,' I say, staring into his eyes.

'I love you. I've wanted nothing more in my life,' he whispers.

'I want you to mark me, Ryker. It's time the world knows I belong to you and you, alone.

'Are you sure you are ready?' He asks as his eyes glisten longingly into mine.

Ryker pulls me on top of him, so I sit fully on his lap. He caresses my back as we kiss with intense passion.

'Ryker,' I whisper.

'Astrid,' he whispers. He grazes the spot on my neck, readying himself to mark me, and bites down with his protruded fangs. An overwhelming sense of love and euphoria rush through my body.

My fangs protrude, and I hover over the marking spot on Ryker's neck before biting down on his skin. Intense drowsiness overwhelms me. I bite into his nape, marking him before slumping into his chest and instantly falling asleep.

The sun shines on my face, and hearing the chirping birds outside the window wakes me. Feeling euphoric, only my neck aches where Ryker has marked me. I sit up slowly, rubbing my neck.

'Good afternoon, my beautiful Luna,' he says, smiling, sitting on the edge of the bed.

'Is it really afternoon? Did I sleep all day?' I ask, surprised. Ryker laughs.

'You've been asleep *for two* days,' he smirks.

'What? How did I manage that?' I'm shocked.

'I expected you to be knocked out for a couple of days after marking you,' he smiles. I lift my legs out of bed to stand up, and he races over to me.

'Where do you think you're going?' He asks and wraps his arms around my waist and kisses my neck.

We snuggle up on the bed. I rest my head and hand on Ryker's chest.

'It feels so right to be with you. It feels so good. Words can't express how much I love you. The thought of not being with you hurts me so much,' I confess.

'I feel the same way, Astrid, and wish I could keep you in my arms forever,' he says, kissing the top of my head. Knowing I need to see how all my pack members are going, I have my shower and dress for the day.

When I look at my cheeks in the mirror afterwards, they have a nice red tinge, and my green eyes seem more apparent and brighter somehow. I feel amazing for the first time. I feel safe and loved. Giggling, we waltz down the stairs like two giddy teenagers in high school. I sit on his lap in the dining room while we feed each other.

'I can't believe how cute you two are,' Mia gushes, taking a seat facing us.

We blush and giggle. Ryker gives me a huge grin before quickly pecking me on the nose.

'It's so good to have our Luna home,' Seth smiles.

'It sure is,' Ryker says, kissing and nuzzling my neck. I can't stop squirming and laughing. It tickles so much.

'Ryker, stop it. It tickles,' I plead, between laughs. He pulls me closer and kisses me on the cheek. Everyone in the dining room is extremely happy for us. We finish our meals with much joy and love floating around the table.

'What happened to Alice and Vanessa?' I ask. Everyone pauses and waits for Ryker to explain.

'After what they did and tried to do, I couldn't kill them. I couldn't release Alice and Vanessa without monitoring them, though. Now that Alpha Zenith and her sons are dead, Alice is a shell of her former self. I think that's punishment enough for her. Vanessa is more upset about losing her brothers, more than anything. I gave them the options of staying in the cell indefinitely or returning to their old pack territory to help upkeep the land. Alice is no longer Luna, so she has no power or authority. They're also not allowed to leave the territory without my permission,' he explains.

'Hayley and I are thinking of moving there, so we can monitor Shady crest for you and Alpha Ryker,' Kane says.

'That's a good idea. Who knows what trouble Vanessa and Alice may cause in future? I'm glad. I won't have to walk on eggshells around them. Now that I have my wolf, I can defend myself. They won't be a threat to us anymore,' I say.

Everyone nods in agreement and smiles.

'What are the plans for the rest of the day, Alpha?' Kane asks.

'Our Luna and I have some work in the office we need to start,' Ryker says. I smile.

'Really?' I say, excited.

'You're Luna now. We do everything together,' he says with a beaming smile. I wrap my arms around his neck and nuzzle his mark.

'How are you feeling?' I ask, referring to his mark.

'I feel happier than I have ever felt.' He smiles. 'How are you feeling?'

' I mean your mark.' I laugh.' I'm a little tender from it, but I'll be fine in a few days,' I assure him.

Finishing our breakfast, we go upstairs to his office. Ryker pulls up an extra chair next to me and sits. He places a stack of clean A4 paper and some pens on the desk in front of me.

'We need to write to all the packs informing them Shady Crest is now our territory, and you're now our Luna,' he says. He writes the first letter before I copy everything he has written on a few more bits of paper. I write names and addresses on envelopes and enclose our letters inside them.

'All done!' I say, smiling.

'It's getting dark. Do we want to let our wolves out for a run?' He asks.

'Yeah, let's go!' I grab his hand and lead him downstairs, running out the front door excitedly, removing all our clothes and shifting into our wolves. I lunge at Ryker, and we roll over dramatically. I nip at his face, and we bolt toward the woods playfully together. We play like a couple of puppies: nipping, yapping and nudging each other. We keep running until we find a lake and come to a halt. I jump into the water full speed ahead. Then, in human form, I stand up in the water and flick my hair back in a wet wave high above my head.

Ryker's wolf is staring at me from the bank. The water reaches up to my shoulders. Ryker jumps full speed ahead into the water, splashing me.

'Ryker!' I yell, grinning excitedly. He lingers under the lake's surface before bobbing up again in human form.

We stare into each other's eyes and kiss.

He pulls me against his chest and holds me, stroking my back.

Jazz Ford

'You're amazing,' he says. I look up at him.

'No, babe. You're amazing,' I say, my eyes twinkling.

CHAPTER 25

Three months later,

Gently waking Ryker up, I cover his handsome face in kisses.

'I don't want to wake up,' He murmurs. I throw a pillow at his face.

'Hey!' He sits up and throws a pillow back at me. I lean backward, dodging the pillow. I poke out my tongue: 'Ha! You missed!' I tease.

'Oh, did I?' He says, jumping out of bed and running toward me, flinging me over his shoulder and whirling us around in a circle.

'Ryker! Stop!' I giggle.

'You'll make me sick,' I say. Ryker stops.

'Well, you're no fun!' He feigns a pout.

'No fun? We are always having fun,' I state.

'True.' He says, lifting me over his shoulder. Ryker runs into the dining room downstairs with a grin on his face. I scream his name the whole way down. 'Ryker!' I yell, trying not to laugh at his playfulness. Finally, he sits in a chair and pulls me onto his lap.

'There, I put you down,' he says, winking at me. I roll my eyes.

'Did you roll your eyes at me, Luna?' he laughs.

Everyone at the table eats silently, smirking and trying to contain themselves at our antics.

'Since we have the day off, I'd like to take you into town and spoil you,' he says, nuzzling his face into my neck. I nod in agreement and kiss his cheek. We finish breakfast and make our way to the shopping strip.

'Where would you like to go to first?' He asks. I look around at all the shops and can't help looking at the ice cream shop.

'Ice cream!' I yell, dragging him across the road.

'Ice cream? We just ate breakfast!' He replies.

'I know, but you said you wanted to spoil me today, and it's been so long since I've had ice cream,' I say, pondering all the flavours I might choose.

'Ice cream it is!' He says. I squeal with excitement.

'Yay! Thank you!' I say, wrapping my arms around him.

Entering the ice creamery, a lovely shop assistant named Maisie greets us.

'Alpha. Luna. How can I help you?' Maisie asks. I look at the wafer cones and the different ice cream flavours in the glass cabinet.

'I'll have the triple-scoop cone: one scoop of chocolate, one scoop of mint, one scoop of vanilla, and one scoop of the rainbow, please. Make it massive!' I tell Maisie. I surprised Ryker with my order.

'Astrid, that's a lot of ice cream for a werewolf,' he says, his hands in his pockets, as he waits patiently. Maisie scoops four different flavours of ice cream into a wafer cone just for me.

'I can't help it. I'm so hungry,' I say, folding my arms against myself as I lean against the glass, watching Maisie add the last scoop of the rainbow to my wafer cone.

'Here you go, Luna. That's yours,' Maisie smiles. I'm instantly in a cheerful mood, taking the ice cream from her. I bite into it without hesitation.

'Thank you so much, Maisie,' I say, happily skipping out of the store. I sense Ryker rolling his eyes at me behind my back.

'I saw that!' I laugh.

'Saw what?' He asks.

'You rolled your eyes at me,' I say.

'How do you know?' He asks.

'I don't know. I just know that you did it,' I say and continue to eat my ice cream.

'Where should we go next?' He asks, licking grooves into a scoop of chocolate ice cream in his single-scoop cone.

'Medley's clothing store. I need some new jeans and stuff,' I smile.

All the ice cream in my cone has already gone, leaving the cone with its chocolate-filled point to be devoured.

'Okay,' he says, smiling. I wolf down my cone, savouring the rich chocolate end, and enter the store.

'Alpha, Luna: it has been a while since I've seen you both,' Medley smiles.

'It has been a while, Medley. We have been very *busy*,' I say, smiling coyly at Ryker.

'Of course. I can imagine all the paperwork you have, now that Shady Crest is your territory,' she says, smiling.

'Yes, the paperwork has been insane,' Ryker laughs.

'I'm after some new clothes. All my others don't seem to fit as comfortably as they used to,' I explain.

'You might be interested in our new range over here,' Medley says, pointing to a wall of clothing that has just arrived.

Walking over to the new arrivals, I grab a pair of jeans and a shirt I like and hold them in front of my figure in a mirror.

'This dress is nice,' Ryker says, passing me a dress to try on. I enter the changing room, lock the cubicle door, and push my legs into skinny blue jeans. I almost fall over trying to do the zip-up.

'Are you okay in there?' Medley asks.

'I think there's something wrong with the size, Medley. They don't fit.' I walk out of the change room in a shirt and skinny blue jeans. The shirt is extremely tight around my bust and my tummy, and the zip and the button on the jeans won't fasten. Medley and Ryker giggle.

'Why are you laughing?' I ask. They cannot contain their laughs.

'I love the shirt, babe,' Ryker chuckles.

'But it doesn't fit,' I say.

'I'll see what else I can find you,' He asks with a cheeky look. I roll my eyes and go back into the change rooms.

'I saw that!' Ryker says.

'Saw what?' I ask.

'You rolled your eyes at me,' he says. I can't help but laugh.

'Okay, okay,' I mumble, locking the cubicle door behind me. Ryker tosses some clothes over the cubicle door.

'Try these.' He says.

I put the dress on that Ryker chose: it's stretchy and strapless and sits mid-thigh, exposing a lot of leg.

'This fits much better,' I say, showing him. He eyes me up and down with approval and pins me against the shop wall to kiss me. Our display of affection exceeds what's acceptable in a shop setting.

'Should I leave?' Medley asks, her face a rosy, embarrassed, pink hue. We giggle and blush.

'I'll just be in the office out back if you need me,' Medley yells out, leaving us quickly and tottering off to her office.

We choose more clothes, and I try them on. I place the new clothes I want on the counter, ready to pay, and ding the bell on the desk. Medley totters back out, scans the items, and puts them into a shopping bag. I'm happy to have clothes that will fit me.

'Let's go for a run!' I say as we leave the store.

'Sounds good,' Ryker smiles.

We reach the woods and leave the shopping bags and my new clothes by a large tree. We undress, and I stuff our clothes in the bag with the new items. Ryker shifts into his wolf and runs off. He pauses when he realises I'm not following him. *'Astrid? You haven't shifted. Are you okay?'* He mind links.

'I don't know. I can't shift. Nothing is happening. Why can't I shift?' I mind link back with apparent panic in my voice. Ryker shifts back and dresses.

'It's okay. You're probably just too tired,' Ryker says, kissing my forehead. I shake my head.

'I don't feel tired,' I reply. Ryker takes my hand.

'Come on, let's go home,' he says, and I nod and follow for a while before stopping.

'Astrid?' He asks. I run to the closest bush and throw up.

'Let's go home. I'll call the doctor,' Ryker says, concern in his voice. My surroundings spin and I feel faint before collapsing and blacking out.

I hear the sounds of hospital machines beeping and whirring. I open my eyes and put my arm up to cover them from the bright lights.

'Am I in the hospital?' I ask.

'Astrid. You're awake!' Ryker says, taking my hand and smiling.

'You blacked out. I brought you straight to the hospital. The doctor will be here shortly to speak with us. They took some blood to run some tests. I'm sure you're fine, though. It's just a precaution.' A nurse enters the room with a monitor on a trolley.

'Alpha, Luna: the doctor is on his way. He asked me to get some things set up for him.' she smiles, plugging a machine into the PowerPoint on the wall, switching it on and leaving the room.

'Alpha, it's been quite some time since you've been here,' the doctor smiles.

'Doctor Herman. Is she going to be, okay?' Ryker asks.

'Yes. Astrid will be fine. Her results came back positive. We'll do an ultrasound to see how far along she is.' Ryker and I look at each other, confused.

'Positive for what?' I ask. Doctor Herman chuckles.

'Pregnancy,' he says. My mouth drops open in shock.

'I'm pregnant?' I ask.

'Yes. Congratulations to you both,' doctor Herman says, shaking Ryker's hand.

'I'm going to be a dad?' He asks the doctor. The doctor nods and smiles, squirts some gel across my lower abdomen and glides a scanner device over the gel.

'And there it is,' he gestures to the screen.

Frozen in awe, staring at the medical screen, we see two little arms, two little legs, a body and a head. We can even hear a heartbeat.

'That's our baby?' I ask, looking up at Ryker. His eyes well with emotion as he kisses the back of my hand.

'Yes. That's our perfect baby,' he whispers. Tears of joy and happiness overwhelm me.

'Ryker - we're having a baby!' I cry. Ryker squeezes my hand and kisses my forehead.

'You're going to be the best mother. I just know it,' he says, beaming.

'How far along is she, Doctor Herman? Ryker asks.

'She is twelve weeks, so there'll be no more shifting until the pup's birth,' he explains. He grabs some paper towels and wipes all the gel off my stomach.

'That's why you couldn't shift today,' Ryker ponders. Before I can pull my shirt back down, and after Doctor Herman has finished wiping the gel off my stomach, Ryker kisses my belly.

'You have exhausted yourself, Astrid. I suggest bed rest for a few days. Avoid wearing yourself out. We don't want you collapsing again,' Doctor Herman says. He prints the ultrasound pictures, and Ryker tucks them safely in his pocket before scooping me up in his arms.

'Time to take my family home to rest in bed,' he says, leaning down to kiss my forehead before kissing me softly on the lips. We leave the hospital room beaming.

We arrive back home at the packhouse beaming with our baby news.

Ryker mind-links everyone in the packhouse to come downstairs for an urgent meeting. Mia and Amelia are the first to sit in the dining room. Then, Leon and Seth come running down the stairs frantically. You would think the packhouse was on fire.

'Luna, Alpha. Is everything okay?' Seth pants.

'Take a seat, Seth.' Ryker gestures to the empty chair.

'Now everyone needs to listen carefully. Things are going to be changing drastically around here.'

Mia and Amelia give each other a look of worry.

'What's the cause for the drastic changes around here?' Mia asks.

'Let's just say the drastic changes are for the better, not the worse.' I say.

Ryker takes my hand endearingly. Astrid and I would like to announce we are having a baby. Astrid is pregnant.'

Amelia and Mia jump up off their seats and begin screaming with joy as they race over and hug me tight.

'A baby? You're having a baby?' Amelia asks.

'Yes, I'm already three months pregnant.'

Amelia and Mia scream again while the guys block an ear with one hand and pat Ryker on the back with their other hand, congratulating him.

Jazz Ford

CHAPTER 26

I feel like a beached whale struggling to get out of bed. 'Ryker!' I call out. A moment later, I hear Ryker running up the stairs.

'What's wrong? Is the baby coming?' He asks. I laugh.

'No, we're fine. I just can't sit up. My belly is so huge.' Ryker smiles and walks over to the bed to help me sit up before kneeling beside me and placing his hands on both sides of my belly.

'I can't wait to meet you, little one. It won't be much longer now,' Ryker says, kissing my stomach. Ryker pulls me to my feet, helps me dress, and we walk downstairs for breakfast.

I think twice about sitting on Ryker's lap when I'm as big as I am. Instead, I pull out another chair, breaking our morning routine.

'Wait,' he says, standing and sitting in the chair I have just pulled out. Then, he gestures for me to sit in his.

'You're so sweet,' I say, smiling at him.

'Only the best seat in the house for you, my love,' he says, giving me a wink and a smile.

'Astrid, you must let Hayley and I take you into the city today for baby shopping,' Mia says.

'Okay. Thanks. That would be fun. I need to buy so many baby items.'

Hayley sits in the driver's seat of her car, waiting for us, while Mia helps me hobble down the front steps to the car. I need Mia's help to buckle my seat belt.

'Almost got it,' Mia says, forcing the belt buckle to click.

'If you get any bigger, Astrid, we'll have to buy a seat belt extension,' Mia giggles. We all burst out laughing. *The buckle clicks in.*

'Got it!' Mia yells with excitement.

We stop by Jim's diner on the way for milkshakes and burgers. Although I just had breakfast, I'm constantly hungry and eating for two.

'Do you think it's a boy or a girl? Have you thought of any names?' Jim asks.

'I'm not sure what gender the baby is. I'm excited either way. Ryker and I have thought of a few names. Nothing set in concrete yet,' I say, slurping the last dregs of my blue heaven milkshake. I spin on my swivel seat and look out the window.

'Is something wrong, Astrid?' Hayley asks.

'No, I'm sure it's nothing,' I say, spinning back around to bite into my burger. I can't help but feel I'm being watched. But, of course, Alpha Zenith is dead, so there's no cause for my anxiety.

Shrugging it off, I focus on my food, Jim, baby-talk, the girls, and the shopping we are about to do.

'Now that you've had your second meal today, we should head into town and start shopping,' Mia laughs.

'Okay. Let's fit lunch into that too,' I say. Mia, Hayley, and Jim burst out laughing.

'Go shopping, Astrid, and stop here on your way back, and I'll make you another meal,' Jim says.

'Woo-hoo!' I say, standing up.

'See you in a few hours, Jim,' I say as I shuffle out the door.

We arrive in town and go straight to a baby boutique. There are so many cute clothes to choose from, and not knowing the baby's gender, I restrict myself to shopping for only lemons, greens, whites and greys.

'Look at this teddy bear!' Mia says, hugging it close to her chest. It is a fluffy brown bear with a green t-shirt. It's adorable and soft to touch.

'I think I'll buy this for the baby,' Mia smiles. Hayley comes running over with a soft pink dragon.

'I'm going to buy this for the baby!' She says.

'Oh, look at all these booties!' I squeal, picking up a set of every colour and tossing them into my trolley. There are a dozen different baby bouncers. They all rock and play nursery songs. I chose the bouncer with green leaves printed on the pattern. Next, I add a box of nappies and a few packets of wipes to the trolley. The baby wraps are so adorable. I chose the set with giraffes on them. Then I came across a set with wolves printed on them. I find Mia and Hayley swooning over the baby toys.

There are baby rattles, soft cubes with the alphabet, and more. Not sure what to choose, I close my eyes, grab random items and place them in my trolley. Mia and Hayley laugh at my antics before paying for the items and heading out of the store.

'Next shop?' I say, and the girls nod.

'Let me take everything to the car, Luna,' Mia says. I smile and push the trolley towards her.

'I'll meet you in the next store,' Hayley says.

'I'll see you soon,' Mia says to Hayley.

I walk up the road and tell Mia I need to sit down and rest for a moment.

'There is a park over there. We can sit on the bench seat. I need the bathroom anyway, so I'll go while you rest,' Hayley suggests.

We make our way across the road to the park with the gorgeous, colourful playground and many trees. A large tree provides lots of shade, so I sit underneath it, watching the children playing on the playground in the distance. I place my hand on my stomach.

I can't believe I will have a child soon. I can't wait to meet you, little one.

I hear rustling in the bushes behind me. Before I can turn my head to see what it is. Someone puts their hand over my mouth and drags me backwards. I tried to scream, but someone stuffed a rag in my mouth and they pressed a knife against my throat. A blindfold wraps around my head, and I'm shoved into a car. I spit the cloth out and speak.

'Who are you? What do you want?' I scream. I want to remove the blindfold, but someone quickly cuffs my wrists behind my back. The metal cuffs cut into my skin every time I try to free my hands. 'Please, don't do this!' I cry. They hold a cloth against my face.

Chloroform! A few seconds later, I blackout.

Dizzy and disoriented, I wake to a car door slamming. My belly weighs me down as I try to sit up. Someone opens my door when I hear footsteps. I'm dragged out of the car aggressively. I scream and try to grab onto something. Unfortunately, I'm surrounded by nothing but dirt and stones.

I mind-link Ryker

'Ryker! Please help me!'

'Astrid, where are you? What's going on?'

'Someone kidnapped me!'

'Where are you? Who has taken you? I'm going to rip their heads off!'

'I don't know. Someone snuck up behind me at the park. I never saw them. They knocked me out with chloroform. I couldn't link you until now. They have dragged out me of the car. I'm not sure where I am. Please, Ryker. I'm scared they will hurt the baby.'

'I will find you, Astrid. I'm sending the pack warriors out to search. Hopefully, we can pick your scent up and get a lead.'

'Please hurry, Ryker. I'm scared. I can't shift to fight back.'

'I know, babe. Just try to stay calm. Link me when you know who it is or where you are.'

'Ryker, if anything happens to me, I just want you to know I love you so much, and I have never been as happy as I have been with you.'

'Astrid, don't talk like that. Nothing is going to happen to you! I love you.'

Hearing dirt and stones crunching under my feet, I'm pushed and shoved forward by my captor. I keep asking questions but don't get a reply. Finally, we stop walking, and I'm forced to sit against a pole. They released one of my hands, only to be cuffed again around the metal bar. Someone drags a chair in front of me. They sit down, lean toward me, and remove my blindfold. My face pales when I see my captor.

'D-Dad?' I stutter.

'Did you miss me?' He asks with a twisted grin.

'Dad! Why are you doing this to me? You can see I'm carrying a baby. Please let me go,' I beg.

'I told you I'd make you pay for your mother's death, or have you forgotten?' He says.

'Dad. I didn't kill her. I know that now. It isn't my fault she died,'

'Lies! If you kept still and listened to her, she would still be alive!' He snaps.

'No, Dad. You don't understand! Zenith killed her. Zenith killed mum!' I yell.

'No! A wolf killed your mother because of your incompetence!' He yells.

'Zenith is the wolf! He was in love with mum, and she rejected him!' I yell. Dad lets out a chuckle.

'Has being pregnant mushed your brain? A wolf called Zenith was in love with your mother and killed her because she turned him down?' He says, clearly amused.

'Yes,' I reply. Dad shakes his head in disbelief.

'This will be hard to believe, Dad, but werewolves exist! Zenith was a man who could shift into a wolf! You never knew, but mum was a werewolf too!' I confess. Dad bursts into laughter.

'If that's the case, wouldn't that make you a werewolf?' He asks.

'Yes, it does. I'm a werewolf. That's what Mum was going to tell me on my eighteenth birthday!' I tell him.

'Okay. If you're a werewolf, prove it,' Dad says.

'I can't shift—'

'So, you're confirming you're a liar?' He says.

'No! I can shift, not while I'm pregnant!' I yell.

'Sure,' he says sarcastically.

'You know, you took something away from me that meant the world to me, and now here you are, carrying something that means the world to you,' he says, looking down at my belly.

'You will not hurt my baby?' I say, worried.

'Oh, Astrid. I will not hurt your baby. I'm going to kill it,' he says.

'No, Dad! Please don't hurt my baby! Let me have the baby first, and then you can kill me. Please!' I plead.

Jazz Ford

'You're pathetic and weak, and your baby will be too!'

Jazz Ford

CHAPTER 27

'Ryker! My Dad! He kidnapped me!'

'Are you at your father's house?'

'No, we aren't at his house. I'm in a big, old shed or run-down, abandoned factory. I've never been here before.'

'Leon is bringing me a map. We'll mark all the abandoned buildings and sheds and check each one.'

'You need to hurry. Dad said he would kill our baby.' I hear a ferocious growl through the link.

'I'll kill him if he lays a finger on you or our baby.'

Dad grabs my hair.

'Are you even listening to me? Or are you too busy zoning out?' He yells.

'Ryker is going to find me, and he will kill you for this!' I yell.

'Your precious Ryker, hey, so, he's your baby Daddy?' he says.

'Yes. Ryker is my mate!' I reply.

'Your mate? And what kind of term is that?' He asks.

'The Moon Goddess chose us to be together. We are soul mates,' I say. He smirks and stands, picking the chair up and throwing it. I watch it smash into pieces.

'Please don't. I'm begging you,' I say as Dad approaches me.

He picks up the broken chair leg on the ground and strikes it across my head. He smiles and leaves. Liquid trickles down my forehead, and drops of blood drip from my head onto my lap, but I can already feel the wound healing. Dad returns an hour later.

'How in the world? Where has the wound gone?' He asks. I ignore him. He kneels to inspect me, realising the deep wound on my forehead has healed.

'Impossible,' he mutters as he stands.

He grabs my face tightly.

'How did you do that?' He asks.

'I already told you. I'm a werewolf. We heal quickly.'

He glares at me for a moment. Liquid runs down my legs. My stomach seizes tightly, and I let out a scream.

'Looks like you're in labour,' he laughs. As soon as the contraction finishes, my forehead drips with sweat. I brace myself for the next contraction, letting out a scream, while my dad watches, smiling.

'I'm going to enjoy the look on your face when the baby comes. You won't get to even hold it!' He says as he walks over to an old bench. I hear metal clinking against metal as he sorts through items.

'I think this will do the trick,' he says, holding up a box-cutter knife.

'No, Dad! Please!' I yell and scream with the next contraction.

'Ryker! Hurry! The baby is coming. I'm in labour.'

'You're in labour?'

'Dad will kill our baby as soon as it's born!' I scream with the next contraction.

'There are twenty different abandoned places. We have checked most of them. We should be able to find you any time now. I promise I'll be there soon!'

Dad approaches me, sits on the ground in front of me, and scratches the blade into the concrete to torment me. My contractions are closer together now. My body is almost ready to push.

We're here! I can smell your scent, he links.

I let out a scream with the contraction.

'I can hear you.' He mind-links me. I hear footsteps outside, twenty metres away. Dad hears them too. He opens a long case and pulls out a shotgun. He points the gun toward the door.

'Let her go!' Ryker growls. My Dad chuckles

'Or what?' He says.

'I'll rip your head off!' Ryker warns. My Dad aims his rifle and shoots. He misses.

'We're going to play it this way then, are we?' Ryker says, removing his shirt and jeans and shifting into his wolf. He charges toward Dad. The gun fires. Ryker yelps.

'Ryker!' I yell, watching the blood trickle from his shoulder. Dad reloads his gun.

'Well, I'll be damned. Werewolves exist. Just think of the money I would get if I shot you dead and skin your fur!' He shouts.

Ryker lets out a growl and circles him. Dad keeps the rifle pointed in Ryker's direction. I scream as another contraction comes and briefly averts Dad's attention, giving Ryker enough time to lunge at him. A shot rings out, and Ryker body-slams into Dad, pinning him to the ground. Ryker snarls close to Dad's face, baring his fangs and a mouth full of sharp canines.

'Whoa, steady there, boy...' Dad says, raising his hands in surrender. Ryker bites down so quickly, killing my dad within seconds. Ryker shifts back into human form and runs to me. He removes the restraints from my wrists.

'The baby is coming,' I pant. 'I need to push,'

'You're safe now. I'm here now. Push babe. You can do this!' He says reassuringly. I nod and push during the next contraction.

'I can see the head!' Ryker announces. 'Come on, babe! One more push!' With all my might, I push. The baby slides out into Ryker's hands and wails.

'You did it!' Ryker says, wrapping his shirt around the baby and placing him in my arms. He sits beside me while we look down in awe at our huge but perfect baby boy.

'Wow! He is one big baby,' Ryker says.

'Definitely an Alpha like his Daddy,' I giggle.

'No wonder your belly was so huge!' He says.

'I've told the doctor and the others where we are. We'll have you and our son home soon,' Ryker smiles.

'I can't believe this boy is our son. What are we going to name him?' I ask Ryker.

'What about Magnus? It's a tough, powerful name, and it also means large. Very fitting for a future Alpha. I think so anyway,' Ryker says.

'Alpha Magnus. I like it!' I smile.

'It's settled. Magnus, it is,' Ryker declares. The doctor arrives, and Ryker cuts the umbilical cord. The doctor drives us home to find many pack members waiting outside the packhouse.

'Wow, half of Shadow Crest must be here,' I say, surprised.

Ryker steps out of the car before helping me up while I carefully carry baby Magnus. Ryker clears his throat and addresses our eager pack members.

'I know you're all keen to meet the future Alpha of the pack, but Astrid and the baby need rest after their ordeal.

'It's a boy!' Someone yells out.

'Yes, it's a boy!' Ryker confirms. Everyone cheers.

'A boy! The future Alpha of Shadow Crest!' Someone says. Ryker and I smile at each other.

'Unless you live in the packhouse, please go home. You'll have the chance to meet the baby during the week,' Ryker says. Guests aren't happy about not being able to see the baby wrapped up in my arms.

I sit in an armchair in the living room. Ryker crouches down beside me and strokes Magnus' thick brown hair. Seth, Kane, Mia and Hayley watch on from other sofas as I unwrap him and take him out of his swaddle. Everyone gasps.

'He is twice the size of a newborn wolf-pup!' Seth says, shocked.

'No wonder you were eating ten meals a day, Astrid! It wasn't to feed you. It was to feed him!' Mia says in astonishment. We all burst out laughing at the truth of her words.

'We have named him,' I say excitedly.

'What's his name?' Hayley asks, wide-eyed.

'Well, we wanted a powerful name, he being a future Alpha. He is going to be huge as an adult. So, we've decided on Magnus,' I say with a beaming smile.

'It's perfect!' Mia declares, clapping her hands together, delighted.

'Alpha Magnus. That is a powerful name,' Seth smiles.

'He has your eyes, Astrid. And your hair,' Hayley says.

'And his dad's nose and handsome face,' I giggled.

'Our perfect baby boy,' Ryker says, proudly placing his hand on my shoulder.

Jazz Ford

CHAPTER 28

Amelia and I sit on the porch drinking tea, heavily pregnant with our second babies, while Magnus plays with little Nina. Amelia and Leon's daughter aptly named Nina because she was such a small, tiny baby, and Nina means 'little girl'. I think it's pretty cute. We laugh as little Nina holds a mouthful of water and squirts it into Magnus' face. Then she pokes her tongue out at Magnus and runs away. Magnus chases after her.

'Little Nina and Magnus are the complete opposite of each other. I say it would be interesting to see if the Moon Goddess chooses them as mates?' I giggle.

'I don't know. Every playdate we have, Nina wears poor Magnus out. She is always playing tricks on him. She is so silly and cheeky, and he is so serious and sensible,' Amelia says, laughing.

'I think I need to go to the bathroom,' I say.

'Me too,' Amelia says. We both call out for our mates.

'Ryker!' I yell.

'Leon!' Amelia yells. They both appear.

'Is the baby coming? Are you okay?' Ryker asks, concerned. I place my hand on my fat belly.

'No, I'm fine. But I can't get out of this chair, and I need to go to the bathroom,' I explain.

'Again? This is like the tenth time already,' Ryker laughs.

'Well, next time, you carry the baby, and try not to pee every five minutes,' I joke.

'Okay, okay,' he says, helping me stand and kissing me.

'Leon! I can't get up, and I need the bathroom too,' Amelia says, her hand on her swollen belly.

Ryker and I laugh. Water gushes down my legs. Ryker and I look down at the water puddling at my feet. We smile at each other.

'Are you ready for baby number two?' Ryker asks. I kiss

him passionately on the lips.

'I'm ready for baby number three,' I giggle.

We make it to the hospital just in time.

Doctor Herman tells me to push again. On my third push, the baby slides out.

'It's a boy.' Doctor Herman says.

'A brother for Magnus, I'm so happy,' I say, gazing into Ryker's eyes.

'Astrid, he is perfect. I think you should name this baby.' He smiles.

'Flint, his name is Flint.' I smile.

A few weeks later, Amelia gives birth to a second daughter she names May. Magnus and Nina remain inseparable, even though they both have a younger sibling they could play with.

Kane and Hayley monitor Shady Crest and live there permanently. Alice and Vanessa fled the first moment they got. No one knows where they have gone to.

When Flint is nine months old, I find out I'm pregnant again. It overjoyed Ryker and me when I gave birth to a little girl we named Josie.

Our family is complete, and we couldn't be happier. Nothing could ever come between my family and friends, not even a curse, could it?

'The Alpha Who Cursed his Mate'
Book Two of The Alpha Series

ABOUT THE AUTHOR

Jazz Ford is a wife and mother of three children. She lives in Geelong, Victoria, Australia. Jazz is a former Personal Care Attendant with a background in nursing homes and in-home care. She loves writing full-time from home. In her spare time, she enjoys photography, graphic design, and spending time with her husband and children. Jazz Ford's other works are 'The Alpha Who Cursed His Mate,' 'The Alpha's Mate and The Vampire king,' 'The Alpha King's Mate,' 'Alpha Maximus: The Last Lycan', and 'The CEO', with many more to come. You can find Jazz Ford on TikTok, Facebook and Instagram.

Made in the USA
Las Vegas, NV
06 February 2023